The Ghost of Soda Creek

Ann Walsh

Porcépic Books
Victoria

Second Printing: February 1992

This edition is published by Press Porcépic Ltd., 4252 Commerce Circle, Victoria, B.C. V8Z 4M2, with the assistance of the Canada Council.

Canadian Cataloguing in Publication Data

Walsh, Ann, 1942-
The ghost of soda creek

ISBN 0-88878-292-6

I. Title.
PS8595.A585G54 1990 jC813'.54 C90-091486-6
PZ7.W34Gh 1990

Printed in Canada.

This book is for John (W.)
who doesn't believe in ghosts
but who has always believed
in me

Although the small community on the old Soda Creek townsite exists today much as described in this book, all the characters in the story are my own invention and not in any way based on real people . . . except, perhaps, for the little ghost.

Ann Walsh

Chapter 1

Kelly was the first one to see the ghost. It stood in a corner of the kitchen, beside the refrigerator, eyes big, staring, never leaving Kelly's face. The ghost wore a red dress, all ruffles and lace, and a floppy red velvet bow in her hair, holding back a long, golden ringlet. Under the dress, lacy edges of pantaloons reached down towards tiny boots that buttoned up one side. Her face was pale, not the sheet-white that ghosts are supposed to be, but a healthy paleness with a soft flush of pink across her cheekbones and, perhaps, one or two freckles over the bridge of her nose. She looked as if she had been crying, and she couldn't have been more than two years old.

Kelly took a step backwards, bumping her hip against the kitchen counter. The dishes left to drain in the rack clattered, the sound loud in the early morning silence. Kelly jumped at the noise, but the ghost didn't move, just stood there, reaching out with tiny hands, her eyes large and sad. Just stood there looking little and lonely and lost. Kelly rubbed her eyes, but the ghost didn't go away. She put out a hand to the counter, steadying herself as her knees felt weak and she wasn't sure she could stand up anymore. "I should say something to her," Kelly thought. "But what does one say to a ghost? Hello? How's it going? Hi, there?"

The ghost lowered her hands, still looking at Kelly. Tears filled the large blue eyes, and suddenly she didn't look real and substantial anymore, but watery, misty. Then she was gone. Completely, absolutely gone, as if she had never been there at all.

Kelly took a few slow steps to the kitchen table, pulled out a chair, and sat down heavily. Her heart was beating faster than it should, and she was breathing as if she had just finished a race. She took a deep breath. "I shouldn't react this way," she told herself firmly. "I don't even believe in ghosts."

It was just after one o'clock on a cold December night. Kelly's father slept soundly, his almost-snores sounding familiar and reassuring through his open bedroom door. The rest of the small community of Soda Creek was also asleep; there were no lights in the other four inhabited houses as Kelly glanced out the kitchen window and looked down the main, and only, road.

Kelly was sixteen, and it was Saturday night, actually early Sunday morning. Saturday nights were often quiet for Kelly. Living in Soda Creek, perched on the banks of the Fraser River a good forty kilometers from Williams Lake, the nearest town, she was isolated from the weekend activities of the larger community. Once in a while she'd spend the weekend with a friend in Williams Lake, or have a classmate stay overnight with her, but many weekends she was alone. It was a long drive to town, and the roads could be treacherous in winter, especially the winding gravel road that led down to Soda Creek from the main highway.

Kelly had been in her room working on an assignment for her art class, and she had become involved in watching her sketch grow, the penciled outlines of spring flowers blooming with her watercolours, the white paper coming alive with colour and energy. Realizing that she was hungry, she had pushed the painting aside and looked at her watch, surprised to find it so late. The trip to the kitchen had been to make herself some hot chocolate and get something to eat. She hadn't even been thinking about ghosts, so why would she see one?

"That's peculiar," she thought. "I'm Kelly Linden, mature for my age, sensible—or so everyone says. Not the sort of person to see ghosts at all." She thought briefly about the event that had made her so 'mature'—her mother's death in a car accident three years ago. Her mother: always quiet, but with a way of listening to people, a way of showing her caring through her eyes, her smile. Kelly shook her head, pushing those thoughts away. She had tried to be mature about her mother's death, had taken over many of the household chores, been strong for her father, sometimes listened helplessly as he wept softly late at night, alone.

But she couldn't think about her mother right now. Now she would concentrate on the little ghost and, sensibly, maturely, try to figure out why she thought she was seeing ghosts. The whole thing would make some kind of peculiar sense if the ghost had looked like her mother. She had been using her mother's watercolours, maybe subconsciously thinking of her, just before she walked into the kitchen. But the ghost was a blonde child, not at all like her mother whose heavy, dark hair had framed her face like an ebony curtain. Kelly had envied her mother's hair. Her own hair was wiry and red, very red, and it remained untamed no matter how many cream rinses she used, no matter how tightly she braided it.

The ghost's blonde ringlets fell tidily into place, ringlets that someone had lovingly tied up in soft rags at night, then carefully combed out the next morning and caught back with a red ribbon. The ghost's mother must have used rags for those ringlets because there weren't curlers or electric curling irons in those days.

"Those days?" Kelly spoke out loud, startling herself. "I'm really slow tonight," she thought. "That wasn't a modern ghost. The button boots, the pantaloons—my little ghost comes from history, probably sometime in the last century. Why, she's quite historical."

Historical? Kelly grinned at herself. Well, hysterical maybe. Ghosts didn't have mothers who carefully curled their hair before sending them out to haunt the kitchen of a perfectly ordinary millwright and his almost perfectly ordinary daughter.

Cautiously she stood up and headed for the fridge. No ghost materialized beside it. She took out the milk and put some on the stove to warm, found one of the doughnuts her father had brought home and, firmly putting all thoughts of ghosts out of her head, made hot chocolate and took it and the doughnut to her room.

At her bedroom door, she stopped and looked around her, as if she had never seen the room before. During the two and a half years that she and her father had lived in Soda Creek, they had become fascinated by the history of the place. In the mid-1800's miners searching for gold came by foot or stage coach up the Cariboo road, as far as Soda Creek. There the steam boats waited for them, the big sternwheelers that carried people and freight up the Fraser River to Quesnel. From Quesnel it was just a few days' journey into Barkerville and the gold fields.

Fewer than a dozen houses now formed the tiny community on the original Soda Creek townsite, a handful of houses strung along a gravel road on a narrow bench of land between hills that rose steeply on one side and the Fraser River on the other. But once, Soda Creek had been one of the most important stopping places for travellers along the Cariboo Road. When gold had been discovered in Barkerville, people came to the Cariboo area by the hundreds, all of them with the dream of wealth. And, as the hopeful miners came, so did others—hotel owners, stage coach drivers, saloon girls, blacksmiths, carpenters, barbers and more, many more. Soda Creek grew rapidly during the gold rush days. The narrow dead-end road on which Kelly and her father lived had once been a bustling main street, and the Fraser River, which she could see through the living room window, had been thick with river traffic.

There were five homes inhabited in Soda Creek now, only five. They were not the homes that the early settlers had built, for those buildings had decayed and collapsed, in some cases sliding gently into the Fraser River in musty heaps of rotting wood. The many people who had once lived in Soda Creek were gone too, leaving behind only a few well-weathered headstones in the tiny cemetery on the hill. The people, like the hotels and saloons and stores, had left almost no trace of their presence. Nothing remained of the once thriving town except an old jailhouse. It had somehow survived, and still stood, leaning a bit, its logs weathered silver and its doors and barred windows long since vanished. And Kelly and her father owned it.

Her father had bought the acre or so of gnarled crabapple trees and the old jailhouse that stood in front of the ancient orchard at the same time as he had bought their house next door. He had decided to live in Soda Creek, rather than in Williams Lake, as Gibraltar Mine, where he was soon to begin work, was only a short drive away.

Alan Linden had plans for the old jailhouse. "We're going to fix it up, Kelly, restore it. Turn it into a kind of museum, full of artifacts and things from the days when Soda Creek was booming."

He had begun to work on the jailhouse just the past summer, removing rotting floorboards, re-framing the glassless windows. But after only a week he had abandoned the project. "It's too nice to be working inside," he said, "and, to be honest, the place gives me the creeps when I'm alone in there."

So the collection of Soda Creek relics—oddly shaped and coloured glass bottles, rusty horseshoes, square-headed nails, unidentifiable bits of machinery—that Alan Linden had unearthed as he worked in his garden or explored the steep banks of the Fraser River, were housed in Kelly's room, filling a large shelf over her desk.

Kelly drank her chocolate, now cold and scummed across the surface, and looked at the shelf that held bits and pieces of long gone days in Soda Creek. She had just spent the evening in her room close to those relics; her mind must have been subconsciously full of thoughts of the days when the town was alive, busy. Perhaps that was why she had come up with a tiny ghost who was dressed as if she had just stepped across from the last century.

Kelly sighed, brushing her hair away from her forehead. In spite of her rationalizing, she couldn't get rid of the image of that tiny, lost figure reaching out, her pleading, enormous blue eyes filling with tears.

She picked up a pencil and tore a fresh page from her sketchbook. Then, at two o'clock on a Sunday morning in December, the wind complaining around the house, muttering in the trees, Kelly began to sketch a small, lonely figure with golden ringlets and high-button boots.

Chapter 2

When Kelly awakened the next morning, the sun was streaming through her bedroom windows, the wind had stopped complaining around the house and the clock by her bed said nearly nine o'clock. "Forgot to close the curtains last night," she thought, and rolled over, away from the sunlight. Eyes tightly shut, she tried to drift into sleep once more, not wanting to get out of bed just yet. She was nearly asleep again when she heard the doorbell ring.

She listened for her father's footsteps, relieved when she heard him heading for the front door. Kelly didn't feel at all like struggling out of bed and answering the door. When she first woke up her hair looked wild, strange, and she'd seen the expression on people's faces when they saw her first thing in the morning.

There were voices in the kitchen now, her father's comfortable rumble and another voice—man or woman's, she couldn't tell. Well, whoever it was planned on staying for a while, because she could hear her father offering coffee. She shut her eyes and tried to ignore the sounds from the kitchen.

She wondered again who the visitor was, then her thoughts drifted away, back to when she and her father had first moved to Soda Creek, two and a half years ago. It hadn't taken them long to realize that their new community seemed to be almost in a state of war.

Their first visitor the July day they had moved into the log house overlooking the Fraser River had been Clara Overton, a home economics teacher at the high school in Williams Lake. Miss Overton was 'overdone' in every way: overweight, overly thick make-up that cracked and crinkled around her eyes, over-elaborate, gaudy clothes and too much flashy jewelry, including an enormous charm bracelet which she wore all the time. When she talked, Miss Overton seemed to put some words in capital letters, and they jumped out of her sentences, startling her listeners. She taught crafts and cooking, and that first morning she had brought a fresh rhubarb pie, topped with whipped cream. Kelly and her father had served coffee and put away two slices of the pie each while they politely answered the teacher's questions—yes, they came from Ontario, Alan Linden was a millwright and had a job at the big Gibraltar Mine, Kelly's mother had died last December in a car accident, yes, it was a dreadful shame, no, they were managing quite well and were both learning to handle housework and cooking. After Miss Overton had offered to teach Kelly the "BASICS of good cooking," and Kelly and her father had shared a smile, thinking of their standard supper—*Kraft Dinner*—the teacher proceeded to tell them everything they needed to know about their new neighbours in Soda Creek. Everything they needed to know, and a lot of things they didn't want to know.

The teacher had shifted several pounds of charm bracelet up her arm and, jangling as she gestured, told them about the 'old timer', Mr. Crinchley, "and you have no idea what an OBNOXIOUS person he is. He has lived alone all his life, and his house, well he never lets anyone into it, but even from outside it SMELLS! His personal hygiene too, well, without going into details I feel sure that he SELDOM bathes. And, he steals fish from our NATIVE brothers!"

Alan had looked puzzled at the last statement and the teacher explained that, in summer when the spawning salmon head up the Fraser River, the Indians are allowed to 'dip' them from the river. Catching spawning salmon is illegal for white people, she went on to explain, but Mr. Crinchley had, for many years, supplemented his old age pension by dipping dozens of the fish and selling them to people in town. "The locals call those salmon, 'Fraser River turkeys'. And Mr. Crinchley had a long list of regular customers, including some in the TEACHING profession! He was extremely unpleasant when someone reported him to the Fish and Wildlife department, and they came and took his nets and gave him a LARGE financial penalty as well. He has been positively UNCIVILIZED to his neighbours since then; he suspects that someone here reported him, and he has hardly spoken to ANYONE in Soda Creek for years."

Shortly after Miss Overton left, with promises to keep an eye on Kelly and give her a "mature, FEMININE role model", Mr. Crinchley himself arrived.

"Good to see some new faces," he said, holding out a pint jar of a murky pinkish substance. "Here. House-warming. Smoked salmon. I smoke it myself, process it too." He turned down Miss Overton's rhubarb pie with a snort, and then started his own commentary on the inhabitants of Soda Creek.

"This used to be a fine place to live, back 'till some of them folks moved in. I ain't set foot in another house in Soda Creek in years. That Overton woman, she's a sneak and a gossip. Wouldn't be surprised if it weren't her that reported me to Fish and Wildlife. Nothing wrong with a man making a bit extra on the side. Why, the Indians from the Soda Creek reserve, just down the road, why they sell those turkeys all summer long, and they ain't supposed to. 'Course, when a white man does it, it's worse, somehow. Oh, I still dip me a couple or so, like that jar I gave you, but there ain't no percentage in taking any to town to sell, now that the wardens keep their eyes open for me."

It was Ed Crinchley who had explained to Kelly and her father about Soda Creek's name. "It's a real creek around here," the old man said. "The water in it comes out fizzy, sort of like soda water. It's the soil or limestone rocks or something that causes it. There's supposed to be a 'whiskey creek' nearby, too—whiskey to go with the soda, you know—but I ain't ever heard of anyone finding it, though I bet there's many who have gone looking!"

Before he left, Mr. Crinchley, like Miss Overton, had complained about everyone else in the small townsite of Soda Creek. There were the Terpens, Mr. and Mrs., and their twins, Tommy and Trisha. According to Ed Crinchley, the twins were 'hellions'. (Clara Overton had called them 'DISRUPTIVE children'.)

"Up and down the street all hours of the day and night," explained the old man. "Sneaking about in them empty houses, screeching and running that dirt bike past my windows so loud my eardrums are like to burst." He had muttered something about some people not being allowed to have children, then turned his attention to the remaining inhabited house in the neighbourhood. "That little brown place at the end of the road, the one with all the flowers and the big vegetable garden, there's two fellas live there. Alone, if you get my meaning."

Alan quickly discovered that he had to start another pot of coffee, turning his back on the old man's commentary.

Shortly after Mr. Crinchley had left, muttering something about cows and a bunch of 'hippies' down at the old ranch, the two 'fellas' he had spoken of arrived at the Lindens' front door, smiling shyly when Alan opened it. Ben was very thin, with wiry, strong arms and long hair that waved gently around his neck. Bob had thick, curly dark hair, shorter than Ben's, and without actually being plump, gave an impression of 'roundness'. They were both about Alan Linden's age, in their forties, and they spoke together.

"We just wanted to say 'hi', and welcome to Soda Creek. I'm Ben Gibson and. . ."

"I'm Bob Lalonde. We're so pleased that you have. . ."

"Go ahead, Bob, you were first."

"It's okay, Ben, I interrupted you." They smiled at each other, and then again at Kelly and her father.

"I've brought you a housewarming gift," said Ben. "Fresh butter lettuce, and a special variety of white radish that I'm trying this year. Gardening's my hobby."

"And I brought a wall hanging, done in yarn, you know, crewel work. I do some pottery too, but I thought you might prefer something bright to hang on the wall."

They had stood there, side by side on the front porch, holding their gifts out in front of them, tentatively, almost as if they were unsure of their welcome.

"Thanks, that's very thoughtful. . ." began Alan, but Kelly had caught sight of Bob's gift and she interrupted. "Can I see that please?" she asked, taking the wall hanging as her father ushered Ben and Bob into the house. The hanging Bob had brought showed a sunflower, glowing with shades of thick yellow yarn, reaching across the canvas as if it were stretching for the sun. "This is great," she said. "I tried this embroidery, crewel work once, but I'm terrible at it, at the embroidery part anyway. I can get the patterns, and I know how I want the finished thing to look, but I can't make the stitches behave."

"Kelly wants to be an artist," said her father, proudly. "She's planning on going to art school one of these days."

"Bob paints too," said Ben. "He has his own studio in Williams Lake where he sells his pottery and crewel work and paintings."

Over coffee and what was left of Clara Overton's rhubarb pie, Kelly, at Bob's request, had brought out her sketch book and her few finished watercolours. Ben had gone immediately for a pile of seed catalogues on the coffee table, grinning at Alan as he said, "Another gardener! Great."

Ben and Bob had stayed for an hour that first day,

Bob, his head bent over Kelly's sketch book, suggesting a small change in line here, showing her where to darken a shadow somewhere else, while Ben and Alan spent the visit deep in discussions of soil acidity, hydroponic gardening and the new hybrid plants featured in the seed catalogues.

"Soda Creek has a gentle growing climate, the best growing climate anywhere in the Cariboo," Ben explained proudly, almost as if he were personally responsible for that phenomena. "It's a sort of micro-climate, caused by the protection of those hills behind us and the moisture and warmth of the Fraser River."

Kelly had looked up from her sketch book, surprised. "The first time I saw Soda Creek, with the hills so close and so steep, I felt that, that 'protection', I mean. I thought somehow of the hills being a large animal like a lion, with the town nestled right beside it as if it were being protected, like a lion cub. I hadn't thought about Soda Creek being *really* protected so that things grow better. I just saw it that way and thought I would like to paint it sometime."

"Ben complains about that hill starting practically in his greenhouse," said Bob, "but he doesn't complain a bit when he wins all those prizes for his vegetables and flowers at the Fall Fair every year. And just look at the crabapple trees in your orchard. No one has pruned them or sprayed them or even watered them for years, but they produce a huge crop every season just the same."

As their new neighbours were leaving, Kelly had been surprised to hear Ben tell her father that he would have to put a good, strong fence around his garden if he wanted it to survive. "Dogs?" asked Alan.

"I wish it were just dogs. Cows. And the twins. There's a 'commune' place on the old homestead at the end of the road, city people, only been here a few years. Sort of aging hippies."

Bob laughed, "They're okay, Ben, but they're just learning how to run a farm."

"They don't know the first thing about handling livestock. That fence is always down somewhere, and the cows wander through the town and into our gardens. And they're much more difficult to clean up after than dogs!"

"And what about the twins?" asked Kelly, remembering both Ed Crinchley's and Miss Overton's horror stories about those children.

"Oh, they're not too bad, really," said Bob, again laughing. "It's just that one year they took the heads off every one of Ben's tulips, just as they were about to bloom. He has never forgiven them."

"They ate them!" added Ben, horrified. "Ate every single bud."

Kelly and her father had looked at each other when Ben and Bob left. "Well, Kelly?" asked Alan. "Are we going to like living in Soda Creek?"

"I don't know, Dad. It looks as if our home is the only neutral zone in a community war. It could be interesting, but. . ."

Two and a half years later, Kelly lay in bed on a Sunday morning and thought about how some things had changed since her first day in Soda Creek, but how most things had stayed exactly the same. She knew everyone else who lived in the old townsite fairly well by now, except the group from the commune who smiled and waved as they rounded up their errant cows, but always seemed too busy to stop and talk; Clara Overton who continually found excuses to "pop over with a little something SPECIAL for your dinner," and who had begun to flirt outrageously with Kelly's father; cantankerous Ed Crinchley, whom Kelly had discovered was called 'the Grinch' by almost everyone in Soda Creek, who would spend long hours with Alan Linden, grumbling about his neighbours or telling stories of his life in Soda Creek. The twins, Tommy and Trisha, now nine years old but still very active, were often found at the Lindens' front door, chorusing, "The clutch on the ski-doo is jammed, can Mr. Linden come and help us?" The twins' parents, the Terpens, also visited, sharing child-raising experiences with Alan—"We believe in permissive parenting, but. . ." Ben and Bob seldom missed a Sunday morning visit to the Lindens, Ben and Kelly's father burrowing through seed catalogues or, in the growing season, inspecting seedlings and comparing notes on fertilizers and mulches, and Bob talking to Kelly about his latest pottery project or a new crewel design, always asking to see Kelly's current art projects.

Kelly's first intuitive guess, that the Linden home was the only neutral place in the community, had turned out to be correct; no one in Soda Creek visited any of their neighbours—except the Lindens. Even the Shuswap Indians from the Soda Creek Band, who had so little to do with the white community, would call Alan for help with their cars, water pumps or other malfunctioning machines. The group from the commune, too, came to Alan when they needed help, although they avoided the other townsite residents, uncomfortably aware of the harsh feelings over their wandering cows. They had added bee-keeping to their homesteading activities, and Mrs. Terpen, whose twins were allergic to bee stings, had been outraged.

Everyone came to Alan Linden for help, for conversation, for friendship. And he gave it freely, laughing as he repaired Ed Crinchley's toaster so it would 'give the blasted bread back', changing the oil in Ben and Bob's car, replacing the motor in Clara Overton's washing machine or the broken chains of the twins' bicycles. He supplied enough crabapples from the old orchard behind the jailhouse for the Grinch's crabapple wine, Miss O.'s Christmas jelly, and the tart apple sauce the twins loved, and allowed the group from the commune to gather the bruised windfalls for their livestock. He listened and he helped. He lent his tools, his skills, his time, and he filled his weekends with people.

When they had first come to Soda Creek, only months after her mother's death, Kelly and her father had found a comforting Sunday morning routine for themselves. They would sleep late, make a large breakfast, then spend the rest of the morning at the kitchen table, refilling their coffee mugs and talking. Talking about their week, about the funny or sometimes serious happenings at Gibraltar Mine, about Kelly's school, her new painting, her friends. And they'd talk about her mother, too; quietly, without tears, exchanging memories, reminding each other of things that had been said, things that had happened, times they had shared when they were a whole family, when her mother was alive.

Sunday morning together, just Kelly and her father, had been a ritual that Kelly suddenly realized that she missed desperately now, for it had been over a year since they had been alone on a Sunday morning. Somehow, people had started coming over for coffee, often before breakfast, staying to share bacon and eggs, others arriving as soon as the first visitors left, staying through lunch, and still others arriving on their departure, often not leaving until evening. Her father sat there smiling, sharing, doing minor repairs right on the kitchen table, listening, giving his Sunday to these people who wouldn't even all come and visit at the same time so it would be over and done with, but who drifted in, one group after another, careful not to run into their other neighbours.

Kelly sat up in bed, now fully awake and back in the present. "It isn't fair," she thought. "Just because they don't like each other and won't speak to each other, they expect Dad to be available all weekend." She still heard voices from the kitchen, and felt herself growing angry. Well, this Sunday morning was going to be different, was going to be like the first Sundays she and her father had spent in Soda Creek. She would get rid of whoever was with her father, then she'd fix breakfast, and she and her father would sit and talk, just the two of them.

Hair quickly braided, the stubborn bits at her temple tucked under a green ribbon headband, Kelly pulled on her clothes and walked, none too quietly, to the kitchen.

Clara Overton was sitting at the table, close to Alan, one hand clutching his sleeve, the other flourishing a wilted handkerchief.

"Oh, Alan," she said, ignoring Kelly, "It was SO frightening, SO upsetting. . ."

"Dad," Kelly interrupted, speaking over Clara Overton's head, "Dad, let's have breakfast by ourselves this morning, the way we always used to."

"Kelly," said her father, a warning in his voice.

"Clara is very upset."

"But she's been here for ages," Kelly hissed in a half whisper, not caring if the teacher heard. She pulled out a chair and sat down on the other side of the table, her eyes not leaving her father's face.

"Kelly!" her father said again, this time his meaning unmistakable.

Kelly sighed. "Okay, Dad. Sorry," but a small voice inside whispered to her that she wasn't the least bit sorry, and maybe Miss O. would take a hint and leave.

Clara Overton dabbed at her eyes with the handkerchief, smearing mascara down her cheeks. "Oh, Kelly," she said. "You don't know how lucky you are to have such a STRONG man for a father. I have such a DELICATE nature, and I desperately need his SUPPORT this morning."

Kelly reached for the coffee pot. "Stupid woman," she thought. "I'll bet the Grinch snarled at her." She squeezed out a small, artificial smile. "I'm so sorry, Miss O. What happened?"

"Oh, Kelly," Clara Overton reached across the table and grabbed Kelly's hand. "Oh, Kelly, you won't BELIEVE it. Last night I saw a GHOST!"

Chapter 3

Kelly didn't react for a few seconds, and Clara Overton repeated herself, her long fingernails digging into the back of Kelly's hand as she spoke. "A ghost, Kelly, a most upsetting, FRIGHTENING apparition."

Shaking off the woman's clutching hand, Kelly moved to the stove, replacing the coffee pot. As she set it down her hands shook, rattling the pot against the chrome ring of the element. She had pushed the thought of the little ghost to the back of her mind. Now this ridiculous woman sat in the kitchen, clinging to Alan Linden's arm and blithering about apparitions.

As politely as she could, Kelly forced a smile and said, "Oh? I didn't think anyone believed in ghosts anymore."

"Oh, Kelly, I don't you know, not really, but I get these FEELINGS sometimes, and when I saw her standing. . ."

"Her?" Kelly spoke sharply. "What kind of a ghost

do you think you saw, Miss Overton?" She glanced at her father, hoping to see him share a smile with her, give her some signal that he was as irritated by this hysterical woman as Kelly herself was, but his face remained serious.

"Clara said it was a child, or the ghost of a child," he said. "She saw it about three this morning."

"But I saw it first," thought Kelly, irrationally. "What did your ghost look like, Miss O.?" she asked, her voice too loud.

"It was a GHASTLY sight, simply horrible. It had the whitest face, and it stretched out those tiny arms as if it wanted to grab me!"

"A child ghost? How old was she?" Kelly was upset, and could barely keep her voice from shaking. If there had been a ghost, it was her ghost. She had seen it first, just after one o'clock, and it wasn't frightening, well, not very much, and certainly not as 'ghastly' as Clara Overton was claiming.

"I think she was two, maybe three years old, and dressed most PECULIARLY. Oh, Alan." She fluttered the handkerchief, turning back to him. "Oh, Alan, you have no idea what a SHOCK it gave me."

Kelly interrupted as Alan placed his hand comfortingly over the teacher's hand, and began to make soothing noises. "Miss Overton," she said, emotion spilling over into her voice so it did shake, "Miss Overton, I don't see how you could possibly be frightened of a ghost who's only two years old. Are you sure there isn't something else bothering you, something else that has upset you so much?"

Kelly's father looked at her in surprise. "Now, Kelly," he said. "Clara's had a shock. You're not being very sympathetic."

A red mist suddenly wavered in front of Kelly's eyes —anger, temper. For years she had heard the old jokes about redheads having violent tempers and had laughed at them, but this morning she felt something uncontrollable moving through her, making her want to shout at the woman sitting beside her father, to scream at her. "Perhaps you should go home and lie down, Miss O.," she said, fighting the urge to pick up her coffee mug and fling the contents at the pudgy, streaked face in front of her. "I'm sure you didn't really see a ghost, but women your age sometimes do get a bit hysterical."

"Kelly!" Alan rose to his feet, his cheeks flushed, and Clara Overton's face went white behind her makeup. "Kelly, that was unforgivable of you. Please apologize to Clara at once, then go to your room. You had no right to speak to her that way."

As quickly as it had come, Kelly's anger evaporated, leaving her trembling and ashamed of herself. "Sorry, Miss O., I'm really sorry. I'm tired this morning. But I am sorry you were frightened by the little ghost. She didn't mean to scare you." Then, before anyone could ask her what she meant, she left the kitchen and went to her room.

She sat at her desk, looking at the picture she had drawn last night. The little ghost stared back at her, eyes wide, pleading, the red velvet bow in her hair looking limp, as if it needed a mother's hand to re-tie it firmly around a ringlet. "What's the matter with me?" Kelly thought. She'd been upset, first because the teacher was with her father, the way someone was always with her father these days, then she'd become angry when she realized that Clara Overton had seen her ghost.

"*My* ghost?" she wondered, studying the picture. "Something about the angle of the arms isn't quite right," said the artist's part of her mind. "She isn't pleading, almost begging with them, the way she was when I saw her." Another part of her mind was cringing, curling up on itself, ashamed. Why had it made her so angry to realize that Clara Overton had seen the ghost too? Ghosts didn't haunt just one person, didn't belong to just one person.

She shrugged her shoulders, and put the picture carefully away in a desk drawer. Last night she had managed to convince herself that the ghost was just her own imagination working too hard. Now she was defending 'her' ghost to the teacher, angry that the woman had been terrified by something so tiny, so lost-looking. How could she be defending something she didn't even believe in?

Her bedroom door was flung open, and her father stood there, his face tense.

"Kelly, what's wrong with you?" he asked, echoing Kelly's own thoughts. "You were downright rude to Clara, for no reason at all. You know how I feel about manners, politeness to adults. You've never behaved like this before. What is going on?"

Much to Kelly's surprise, she began to cry. Her eyelids stung, tears filling her eyes and moving down her cheeks, and her throat seemed to close until she could hardly breathe. "Dad, I. . ." she began, and then she put her head down on the desk and began to cry in earnest. "Everyone's got the weeps today," she thought, not even trying to hold back the sobs. "First the little ghost, although she didn't make any noise crying, then Miss O., and now me."

Her father knelt beside her, his work-roughened hands awkwardly patting her hair. Kelly never cried. She couldn't remember the last time she had been in tears—yes, she could. It was the day of her mother's funeral.

Alan spoke softly. "Kelly," he said, over and over. "Kelly. It's all right, little one. It's all right."

Kelly lifted her head and rubbed a hand across her face. She groped for a Kleenex, found one, blew her nose and tried to stop the tears. "Oh, Dad," she said. "It just isn't fair."

"What's not fair, Kelly?" he asked, taking the damp Kleenex out of her hands, passing her a fresh one. "What's not fair, little one?"

"All those people and that horrid woman and there's always someone here with you and we haven't had breakfast together on Sunday and talked, just the two of us, for a long time, and you're always so busy helping them, listening to them. And besides, it's my ghost. I saw her first, and she wasn't trying to scare or hurt anyone and. . ." Her voice failed her again, a loud sob ending the flood of words.

Alan put his arms around her, pulling her to him. "It's all right," he said again. "It's all right. I think I understand, and I'm sorry, Kelly. I didn't realize."

They stayed that way for a while, the tall, awkward man holding his daughter closely, both of them silent. Then Alan stood up, and took Kelly's hand in his. "Come on, little one. Let's get ourselves some breakfast, just the two of us. You're right. It has been a long while since we've spent any time together."

Kelly grabbed a fistful of Kleenex from the box on her desk. "No one's called me that, *little one*, for a long time," she said. "Not since . . . not since Mom. . ."

Her father squeezed her hand tightly. "No. Perhaps I wanted you to grow up quickly, too quickly. I think maybe I asked too much of you, Kelly. Too much, too soon."

Kelly blew her nose loudly. "Nonsense," she said. "You didn't make me grow up in a hurry. See, I still have temper tantrums and tears. I like looking after the house and you—well, most of the time I do. And I'm still short, too. I haven't really grown 'up' very much at all!"

"Well. . ." her father answered, beginning to smile. "The cooking. I seem to remember an angel-food cake that was only one inch high, and a very special chili when you used cayenne pepper instead of chili powder, and some biscuits that I broke a tooth on."

"Come on, Dad," said Kelly, beginning to smile herself. "It hasn't been that bad. You know your tooth was cracked before you ate my biscuits, and my cooking's been getting a lot better since Miss O.'s been helping me."

At the mention of Clara Overton, both of their faces became serious again. "Kelly, I. . ." Alan's voice was hesitant, "Kelly, I just . . . I mean, I want you to know that Clara is a very unhappy person, and she needs someone to talk to once in a while, but there's nothing . . . I mean, I just feel sorry for her. I don't really even like her very much, so you needn't worry."

It took Kelly a minute to understand what her father meant, but when she did she grinned at him. "It's okay, Dad. I'm not jealous of her, if that's what you're trying to say."

"Um, well, I just thought that maybe you were wondering about Clara and . . . and me."

"I'm not wondering, Dad, but I do hope you don't feel so sorry for her that you marry her!"

Her father stepped back, a strange look on his face. "Never," he said firmly, then repeated himself, loudly. "Never!"

Kelly took a deep breath. "Dad? I guess that is what's wrong with me, partly. I think maybe I am a bit jealous, not just of Miss O. but of all the Soda Creek people. I miss our Sunday mornings, Dad."

"I know, Kelly. I've missed them, too."

"And Dad, the reason I got so angry with Miss O. was. . ."

"Yes?" Her father looked down at her, puzzled.

"Well, because I . . . last night I saw. . ."

Her father waited patiently, but Kelly couldn't go on. "Oh, it's ridiculous really," she said at last. "Here."

Reaching into her desk drawer, she pulled out the watercolour of the little ghost. "I did this last night," she said. "I saw her too."

Her father took the picture and studied it, not saying a word. Finally he looked at Kelly and spoke. "It's Clara's ghost," he said. "It's just the way she described it, the high boots, the red dress, the ringlets."

"But she wasn't trying to frighten anyone, Dad. She wasn't reaching out to grab Miss Overton. She was reaching for something, for someone, for . . . oh, I can't explain it. She's little and alone and very, very sad."

Alan gently placed the picture on Kelly's desk. "I don't understand what's going on here, Kelly. I could understand it if only one of you thought you saw this ghost. Clara is high-strung, and she is at the age when some women begin to get a bit peculiar."

"Sure. That's what I said, and you got angry at me

for saying it."

"Be sensible, Kelly. That's not something you say to a person's face! Clara is very sensitive about her age."

"Sorry, Dad. I know I was rude. But why do you think that *I* saw the ghost, since I'm not at that 'peculiar' age?"

"Well, you were alone last night, up late, and your room is full of things from Soda Creek's past and. . ."

He looked down at the picture again, his forehead wrinkling above his thick, greying eyebrows. Then he shook his head, as if to clear away unsettling thoughts.

"Come on, Kelly. Let's forget about it for now. I don't know about you, but I'm hungry. I'll do the bacon, if you can find that package of pancake mix, and we'll have breakfast together, just like we used to."

"Sure, Dad. That sounds great. Just the two of us, right?"

"Right!" he answered, and then the doorbell rang.

Chapter 4

Kelly and her father looked at each other, and Kelly could feel the tears inching their way back into her eyes. "Well, there goes our breakfast together," she said, trying to control her voice.

"No, we *will* have some time to ourselves today, Kelly," said her father firmly. "I'll see who it is and tell them we're busy. Send them away."

"Sure," said Kelly, unable to make herself believe that her father would be able to do such a thing; trying to believe it, but already seeing their quiet hours together vanishing.

As her father went to the door, Kelly headed for the bathroom to wash her face. After the tears, her cheeks were flushed and her nose seemed almost as red as her hair. She splashed her face with cold water several times, and it seemed to help a bit. In just an hour her hair had curled its way out of the tight braids, and thick tendrils clung to her forehead and cheeks. She retied the ribbon firmly in a band around her forehead, then went out into the kitchen where she could hear her father talking to someone.

"I knew it," she thought. "He hasn't had the heart to get rid of whoever was at the door."

At the kitchen table sat two people, obviously from the commune, although Kelly had not seen either one of them before. Her father, busy filling the coffeepot with cold water, turned as she came in, looking apologetic. "Kelly, this is George and his nephew David from the place down the road. Their pump is frozen and they need a hand getting it going again. Um . . . do you mind if I just run down for a while and have a look?"

"It's okay, Dad. Do what you have to do."

"We'll get that time to ourselves later, I promise. Maybe we can make something special for dinner, or how would you like to go into Williams Lake this evening, and we'll have dinner out?"

"Sure, Dad." Kelly smiled, not as upset as she thought she would be. Dinner out sounded good. At least she wouldn't have any dishes to do afterwards.

"I'm sorry, I didn't mean to upset your plans." George had spoken, and he looked uncomfortable. He had long hair, past his shoulder blades, tied back in a pony tail. He seemed a bit older than her father, late forties she guessed, and he had long, slender fingers that he tapped nervously on the kitchen table.

David was much younger, and even though he was sitting, Kelly could see that he was short, almost as short as she was. He was thin, too thin, and his dark eyes seemed almost too big for his face. His pale skin made the dark circles under his eyes seem drawn there, charcoaled in against the white skin. He looks very fragile, Kelly thought, surprising herself with that word, but then he smiled at her and his face lightened, softened and became almost handsome. "Hi," he said, "where did you get that hair?"

Kelly was startled. People often commented on her hair, but usually they waited until they got to know her, didn't come right out with a question like that the first time they met her. She could see her father watching her, waiting for her to reply, the coffee pot overflowing with cold water now. She smiled at him, reassuring him that she would be polite, then turned back to David.

"From my grandmother, my Irish grandmother," she answered, and heard her father give a small sigh of relief that she hadn't snapped at this visitor the way she had at Clara Overton. Then, suddenly self-conscious, she reached up and tucked a wiry strand back under the headband. "It runs in the family, but it skips a generation. That's why Dad doesn't have it."

"You're lucky," said David. "It's really something."

Kelly found herself blushing. Never in her sixteen years had she thought herself 'lucky'—more like being cursed—with her red, wiry hair. She sat down self-consciously as her father put out clean mugs. "It's an awful nuisance," she said. "But . . . but, thanks."

"Poor Kelly's been called 'red' and 'carrot-top' and all the other names people can dream up for redheads," said her father. "She hates her hair, always has. When she read *Anne of Green Gables,* she ran around sighing for 'auburn locks'. She even dyed it, the way Anne did in the book. Made her look as if she'd escaped from a circus. Her mother cut it off, really short, and when it grew back it had all that frizz to it."

"Dad!" Kelly said sharply, annoyed at him talking

about her as if she weren't there. Then, to change the subject, she asked David, "Have you been here long? With the group at the farm, I mean?"

"Just a few weeks," he answered.

"David's been sick," said his uncle. "Mononucleosis. He's in first year university, or was. Had to take some time off when he got sick. His mother thought the Cariboo air would fix him up, so she sent him up here."

"Hey!" said David, "Do we get to talk about you two now? Come on." He and Kelly shared a grin. "Parents and uncles can be so tactful at times, can't they?" he said, shaking his head.

"Anyway," George went on, hesitant, not sure if he was on safe conversational ground, "anyway, he's much better, and we've been keeping him busy."

"That's an understatement," said David. "I'll have to have a relapse to get any rest. But I've almost learned how to milk a cow. The cows can't wait until I really get the hang of it."

"He's not doing badly—for a city boy," laughed George. "Except he's started seeing things in the barn. Guess the mono's got to his brain."

"Come on, Uncle George, I was only half awake this morning."

"You saw something this morning?" asked Kelly. "What?"

"Well, I really wasn't completely awake, and I was worried about the big cow that likes to kick, so I was distracted, but I could have sworn I saw a little girl in the corner of the barn. I thought at first that it was just one of the kids from our place, then I realized that she was much younger, only about two or three."

Kelly and her father looked at each other in silence. Alan finally spoke. "What did she look like, David?"

"I didn't see too well. The lights in the barn are kind of weak, and it was still dark outside, but she looked as if she was wearing a dress and boots, and she had lots of blonde hair."

"What did she do?" Kelly asked, her voice strained. "Did she say anything?"

"No, she just stood there, didn't make a sound. She had her hands out towards me, and I'll swear she was going to cry. So I turned around, thinking that if she were going to cry maybe I shouldn't stare at her, and when I looked again, she was gone."

"Hallucinations, David," said his uncle. "There aren't any kids under six years old in Soda Creek."

Kelly and her father exchanged looks again, and he shook his head slightly. Another person had seen the child who had visited Kelly, they were both sure of that. But why? As they stood there, silent, while David and his uncle looked puzzled, Kelly realized that there was only one explanation. The ghost was real, uncomfortably but undoubtedly real!

Alan seemed to forget that he had started a pot of coffee. He turned to George abruptly and said, "If we're going to get that pump of yours thawed out and working by evening, we'd better get going." He hurriedly left the room, heading to the basement to pick up his tool box.

George seemed bewildered by this sudden rush to get out of the house, but he picked up the patched denim jacket that he had slung over the back of his chair, and stood up.

David, however, didn't seem at all inclined to leave. "Hey," he said to Kelly, "What about that coffee your dad's making?"

"I'll get you some, if you want to stay for a while." Kelly wanted him to stay, wanted to find out more about what he had seen in the barn that morning, but she didn't want to talk about the ghost in front of George and her father. "Unless you have to help them with the pump."

"I wouldn't know which end of a pump the water comes out of," David confessed. "They won't let me help with that type of work."

"Sure," George said to David, "Sure. You stay here where it's nice and warm and drink your coffee and think of your poor old uncle freezing his fingers off down in the well-house."

"I'll be back as soon as I can, Kelly," called Alan as he headed out the front door. "Perhaps you should show David that picture you drew last night?"

"Picture?" asked David. "You're an artist?"

"Not really," she said, "At least, not yet. I draw a bit, and I'm going to go to art school when I graduate, but I'm not nearly as good as my mother."

"Where is your mother?" asked David. "I haven't seen her yet."

Something inside Kelly turned over and hurt. "She's dead," she answered. "For almost three years now."

"Oh. I'm sorry. I didn't know. I mean, Uncle George didn't say anything. I'm sorry, Kelly." He reached a hand out, as if he were going to touch her, then quickly drew it back. "I . . . I guess I should head out now, maybe I can help with that pump or go talk to the cows or something."

"Don't be ridiculous," snapped Kelly. "There's nothing wrong in you not knowing. Don't worry about it." She clenched her jaw, biting down hard on the hurt inside her, and poured David's coffee. "Besides," she went on, determined to change the subject, "besides, I think we should talk about what you saw this morning."

"What I saw? Oh, the kid in the barn. Well, I guess she must be staying with someone around here and just wandered over. Maybe she wanted to see the cows. Maybe she wanted to watch me try to milk the cows. From the way everyone talks, that's a very funny sight."

"Your uncle was right, David," said Kelly. "There isn't a child under six closer than the reserve, a few miles down the road."

"Who was it then?" asked David, now serious. "She wasn't lost, was she? I didn't mean to ignore her, but. . ."

"Maybe she is lost," said Kelly, "but you couldn't have helped her find her way home."

"What do you mean?" David's coffee sat untouched on the table. "What are you talking about?"

"Don't laugh, David, just answer me. Do you believe in ghosts?"

"Ghosts?" David looked startled. "No. I don't. Or at least I don't think I believe in them. I've never seen one."

"You saw one this morning, David," Kelly said softly. "You saw a ghost this morning."

Chapter 5

About an hour later Kelly and David still sat at the kitchen table, now littered with dishes. Kelly, realizing that she hadn't yet eaten, had produced the pancake mix, but David had actually done the cooking.

"I'm good at pancakes," he said. "Look, no matter what the recipe for the mix says, you always add an egg, and just a bit less water. Like this." He had taken the bowl and mix out of her hands and made himself at home in the kitchen. Kelly had cooked the bacon, only burning it slightly, and located the syrup in the back of a cupboard, while David wielded the flipper on the pancakes. And they were good, Kelly had to admit, better than the ones she usually made.

Now they sat, the sticky plates pushed to one side, staring at Kelly's picture of the little ghost.

"I still can't believe it," David said. "In spite of what you've told me, I still can't really believe it. I always thought that ghosts would be tall white things in sheets, not a little girl looking so real. Maybe we're having some sort of hallucination."

"I don't know, David, but I don't see how that could happen. I mean, we don't have much in common, the three of us who have seen her—you, me and Miss Overton."

"Maybe we should work on developing more things in common then," he said.

Kelly grinned at him, wickedly. "Oh, you mean you would like to get to know Miss O.? Well, I'll be pleased to introduce you."

"Come on, you know what I mean." David looked down at the picture again, hiding his eyes from her. "You and I are the only two around here who aren't over thirty or under ten. I don't know about you, but I've been lonely even in the short time I've been here. Aren't you too? Lonely?"

At his direct question, Kelly's grin faded. "Yes. I guess I am, but I'm at school most of the time, and when I get home there's housework and dinner to get ready, and my painting—and Dad, when I get to see him."

"Well, if you cook all the meals the way you did that bacon, maybe you should spend less time on your painting and more in the kitchen! Your art work is good, but I'm not so sure about your cooking."

Kelly was thinking quickly, searching for a reply to David's remark about her cooking, when, for the third time that day, the doorbell rang. She went to answer it and returned to the kitchen with the Terpen twins trailing behind her.

"David, this is Trisha and Tommy. They live two houses down."

The twins stared at David, then looked at each other and giggled. "Is he your boyfriend, Kelly?" asked Trisha.

"Trisha!"

David looked seriously at the twins. "Of course not," he said. "People with red hair sometimes have very bad tempers. Do you think she'd be a good girlfriend."

"Oh, I don't know," said Tommy. "Kelly's okay, I guess, if you like girls. I think girls are dumb."

"They are not," said Trisha.

"They are too."

"Are not!"

"Are too!"

Kelly stepped in before the argument could become physical, something that happened frequently when the twins had a disagreement. "Come on, you two, stop that. Do you want some orange juice?"

"Sure. You got any pancakes left?" Tommy had inspected the sticky plates and deduced what had been served for breakfast.

"Yeah. We like pancakes, but Mom never makes them." Trisha wiped syrup from the edge of a plate and popped her finger in her mouth.

"There's lots of mix left," David said, standing up. "I'll make you some pancakes if you like, but no arguing while you're here."

The twins solemnly agreed, then sat down, watching and waiting while David once again mixed, poured and cooked. Kelly brought two glasses of juice and set them in front of the twins. "Were you looking for Dad?" she asked. She had always found the twins difficult. Either they both talked at once, loudly, or they both kept silent. Either way, a conversation with them was always a challenge.

"Yes," said Trisha.

"No," said Tommy.

"Well, sort of," they finished together.

It was quiet for a while, the twins anxiously eyeing David's progress at the stove, Kelly wondering what crisis had brought the children to her house this time, and how soon she could get rid of them. The silence continued for what seemed like hours, broken only by David's soft whistling as he flipped pancakes.

"There you go." As he set two plates heaped with pancakes in front of them, Trisha caught sight of Kelly's painting of the little ghost. It had been on the table right in front of the twins ever since they sat down, but they had been too interested in watching David cook pancakes to notice it.

"Look, there she is! See, Tommy, I wasn't lying, neither. Kelly's made a picture of her, so she must be real."

Kelly and David exchanged a glance, and Kelly asked, "Do you know the little girl in the picture, Trisha?"

Tommy answered for his sister, "Naw, she just. . ." The rest of the sentence was unintelligible as he worked on a mouthful of pancakes and syrup.

"Yes." Trisha spoke at the same time as Tommy. "Yes. I saw her last night."

"Did not." Tommy was between bites, his voice loud and clear.

"Did too!"

"Never did. Liar!"

"Did too!" Trisha's voice sounded suspiciously near tears, and Kelly had had all the tears she needed for one day, so she broke in quickly.

"Tommy, please be quiet and let Trisha tell me

about the . . . about the little girl she saw last night. Don't interrupt her."

Trisha shot Tommy a victorious glance, took a swallow of juice to wash down what was left of a mouthful of pancakes and said quickly, "This morning, early, when it was still dark, when I woke up to go to the bathroom, she was there in the hall, right by the bathroom door, and she put her hands out and then she went away and I got Mommy but she said it was a dream." She paused to take a breath, then went on. "So I went to the bathroom and went back to bed and Tommy says I'm a liar but I did see her, I did!"

Kelly sighed. These appearances of the ghost were getting out of hand. How could she explain to a nine year-old child that what she had seen by her bathroom door was most probably a ghost? The twins would be frightened, and their parents would be furious at Kelly for filling their children's heads with psychic nonsense.

Trisha looked at her, her eyes asking for some sort of an explanation, some proof that she had seen a little girl in her house in the early hours of the morning, but Kelly didn't know what to say. It was David who spoke.

"Who do you think she was, Trisha? No, Tommy, let her talk. What do you think the little girl was doing in your house, Trisha?"

Trisha looked triumphantly at the silenced Tommy. "I think it was a little ghost-girl, and she had to go to the bathroom and there aren't any bathrooms where ghosts live so she had to come and use ours," she said, running the words together so quickly that Kelly and David had trouble understanding her.

Tommy, however, understood his sister perfectly

well. "Oh, boy, is that ever dumb!" he said. "That is the dumbest thing in the world. Everyone knows that ghosts don't have to go to the bathroom!"

Kelly was having trouble keeping her face straight, and David had turned his back to the twins, his shoulders shaking with silent laughter.

"Uh . . . well, Trisha . . . be quiet, Tommy . . . Trisha, I think that's a perfectly good explanation. But aren't you afraid of ghosts?"

Trisha answered Kelly seriously. "Well, I guess I would be, sort of, if it were a grown-up ghost, but she's just a little baby and she couldn't make anybody scared."

"Baby ghosts! Boy, that is so dumb!"

Before Trisha could retaliate, David silenced Tommy with a stern look and asked, "Did you tell your parents that you thought you'd seen a ghost?"

Both children looked disgusted. "Naw," said Tommy, and Trisha shook her head, agreeing with her brother.

"They'd just say we were getting hyper . . . hyperaction or something. Tommy and me, we don't tell Mom and Dad about things like ghosts!"

"Yeah. We don't tell them nothing," echoed Tommy.

"Did the ghost-baby come to use your bathroom too, Kelly?"

"Well, she did come to visit me, but I saw her in the kitchen."

"Maybe she was hungry," said Tommy, his disbelief partly suspended as he realized that Kelly was taking the whole business seriously.

"Maybe she was, Tommy. She must have wanted something or she wouldn't have been here."

"Did she go to your place, David?" asked Trisha.

"Mom and Dad say we aren't ever to go to your place because of all the bees," added Tommy.

"Yes," said David. "She came to the barn this morning, while I was milking the cows."

"I wonder why she went to a barn?" said Trisha.

No one had heard Alan return, but he was suddenly in the kitchen, bringing the cold smell of outdoors with him. "Still here, David? Hi, twins. I'm glad you found someone to have breakfast with, Kelly. Anything left? I'm starved."

Once again David headed for the stove. Alan looked amused. "Couldn't stand Kelly's cooking, right, David? I know the feeling. She makes a mean chili, too."

"Oh, Dad, he offered to make the pancakes. I made the bacon."

"And burnt it," David elaborated.

"That's typical."

"Not fair! That's two on one," protested Kelly.

Tommy was again eyeing David as he cooked. "Can we have more pancakes?"

"No," said David firmly. "That's all the mix there is, and besides I'll bet you've already had two breakfasts this morning, right?"

Tommy and Trisha exchanged a guilty look. "We better be going," said Tommy, heading for the door.

"Thank you very much for the delicious pancakes, Kelly, I mean David," Trisha added maturely, and Tommy, by now halfway out the front door, remembered his manners, too.

"Yeah. Thanks," he shouted. The door slammed and they were gone, except for faint voices that drifted down the road.

"Baby ghost, baby ghost, dumb, dumb baby ghost."

"I did see it, Kelly says."

"Dumb baby ghosts. Dumb sisters. Dumb girls."

"Are not."

"Are so."

"Not!"

"So!"

Alan sighed. "Seeing those two always makes me glad you weren't twins, Kelly. I don't know how their parents manage. What did the kids want, anyway? More trouble with the skidoo, or were they just in search of food?"

David put a plate of pancakes in front of Alan. "That is all the mix, Kelly, and you're almost out of eggs and syrup as well."

Kelly answered absently, her thoughts still on Trisha's nocturnal visitor. "Just write it down on the list on the fridge, will you, David."

Alan set down his knife and fork. "She has certainly got you trained in a hurry, David."

David grinned. "Not really," he said. "I'm used to helping with the shopping. Mom hates doing it."

"What did the twins want, Kelly?" Alan asked again.

Kelly shook her head, her forehead creasing as she frowned. "You won't believe it, Dad, but early this morning Trisha saw a little girl by their bathroom door. They were arguing over whether or not she really had seen something, and I guess they came here to get the argument settled."

"Trisha won, but Tommy thinks it's dumb," added David. "As soon as they saw Kelly's picture, Trisha was convinced that she had seen a ghost, just a harmless little ghost girl looking for a bathroom."

"That's as logical an explanation as I've heard yet," answered Kelly's father. "Quite sensible, really. Were the twins frightened at the thought of a ghost running around Soda Creek?"

"No," said Kelly. "Trisha thinks it's just a lost baby, won't hurt anyone, just a lost little girl looking for something or someone. And Tommy just thinks it's dumb."

"Good pancakes," said Alan. He pushed back his chair, stretched, and changed the subject. "You'll have water at your place again soon, David. We put a small electric heater down in the well-house, so it shouldn't freeze up on you again this winter. Been a busy day already, and it's only noon."

Kelly just nodded, suddenly feeling exhausted.

"Ben saw me as I walked back from the commune, Kelly. Came out and talked to me, tried to get me to go in for a cup of coffee, but I'm 'coffeed-out' this morning. Had something he wanted to talk about. Want to take a guess about what was on his mind?"

"I wouldn't be surprised if he thinks he saw a ghost last night," said Kelly, picking up the picture she had drawn. "A little, lost ghost-child."

"Right." Alan wasn't smiling. "Ben will probably be by later to see that picture you drew, Kelly. He was very upset, thought maybe he was going a bit crazy. I told him that you had seen the ghost, too, and that seemed to make him feel better."

"Let's see," said David. "That's Kelly, Miss O., me, Trisha and Ben who have seen it so far. Well, we certainly aren't *all* having hallucinations."

"And it . . . she . . . has to be a real ghost, just because so many different people have seen her. But ghosts aren't real at all." Kelly shook her head, confused.

"This is the strangest conversation I've had since . . . well, this is the strangest conversation I've ever had," said David. "Here we are, sitting around the kitchen table on a Sunday morning, talking calmly, rationally about ghosts."

"I wonder who will see her next?" asked Kelly. "I'll bet that sooner or later she visits everyone in Soda Creek."

"Who else lives here?" asked David. "You are the only people I've met, except for Uncle George's bunch."

"Well, there's Ed Crinchley," said Alan, "but I don't see him ever admitting he'd seen a ghost. He'd just put it down to a bad batch of that crabapple wine he makes."

"And the Terpens, the twins' parents," said Kelly, "but if the ghost has already been to their house, maybe she won't go back. That's it, that's everybody."

"Well," said her father, "there's me and Bob, and there's another dozen people down at the commune—excuse me, David, I don't know what you actually call your place, but we call it the commune."

"They just call it 'the place'," answered David, "but it really is a commune with everyone doing the chores, pitching in to help, sharing whatever money they make to keep the place going. My parents call it a commune, too."

"But Dad," said Kelly, returning to the subject of the ghost, "if she only goes to each house once, then everyone has had their visit, except Crinchley the Grinch."

"Don't call him that, Kelly. He's not nearly as irritable as you think, just a lonely old man who wants to talk but doesn't have much to talk about. So he complains a lot. He'll usually stop, though, if you can get him onto Soda Creek's history; he has a remarkable memory."

"I've never heard him talk about the old days of Soda Creek," said Kelly, surprised. "I've just heard him complain about the twins or the cows or how he can't sell his illegal salmon anymore. Wait until you meet him, David, and you'll see what I mean about him being a 'Grinch'. Anyway, I'll bet he's the next one to see the ghost, if he hasn't already and just isn't talking about it."

Again the doorbell rang, unusually loudly. Kelly, jumped, startled, and even David seemed surprised.

"Another typical Sunday morning at the Linden house," said Kelly's father, sighing. "I wonder who it is this time?"

When Kelly opened the door, she took a step back in surprise. On the doorstep stood an old Indian man, his grey hair caught in two braids that fell almost to his waist, neatly tied with strips of leather. On his head was the tallest cowboy hat Kelly had ever seen, circled by a wide, elaborately beaded hatband. Beside him was a slim woman, not more than twenty-five, her long dark hair falling loose about her shoulders.

"He wanted us to come here," said the woman, gesturing at the old man who stared solemnly at Kelly. "He thought the chief should come and ask about the little white girl who ran away from home last night, the one he thinks he saw in his cabin two hours before daybreak."

Chapter 6

Kelly stood staring at the two visitors, unable to speak for a few seconds. Then she swallowed hard and said, "Won't you come in, please? Perhaps you should talk to my father."

They followed her into the kitchen, and Alan Linden rose to his feet, a smile on his face. "Hi," he said. "We'll put on some more coffee."

Kelly, suddenly embarrassed by the litter of dirty dishes, glasses and mugs, began to clear the table. "Dad, these people want to talk to you."

"Sit down, make yourselves at home," said Alan. "This is David—what is your last name anyway, David?"

"Stanton," answered David.

"David Stanton, and I see you've met my daughter, Kelly. This is Chief Joan and her grandfather, Basil, from the Soda Creek reserve."

"You're the chief?" said David. "But I thought

that. . ." He didn't finish the sentence, not knowing quite what to say, his eyes flickering to the dignified old man sitting regally at the table, his hat in front of him.

"Sure," answered Joan. "There's quite a lot of us, women, who are chiefs now."

"But your grandfather looks. . ." David began.

"I know. He looks like a chief. You should see him when he gets into his outfit for dancing, all feathers and beads and a long spear. Then he really looks like what an Indian's supposed to be." She spoke sharply, with an edge to her voice, and Kelly felt uncomfortable. Her father, watching the exchange, grinned and came to David's rescue.

"Put the coffee on, would you, David? And don't mind Joan. She's a strong supporter of aboriginal rights and she's a fighter, but she doesn't bite on Sundays."

"No. Only on Monday, Wednesday and Friday," said Joan, but this time she smiled, too.

David rinsed and filled the coffee pot as Kelly collected the dirty dishes from the table, stacking them by the sink. Basil took out a small leather pouch and some papers, and began to roll a cigarette, using only one hand. He saw Kelly watching him and smiled. "Only got one hand free when you're on a horse. Learned to do this when I was a kid."

Joan glared at Basil's cigarette, then sighed. "He says he's too old to quit. Do you mind?"

Kelly rummaged in the cupboard and found the one ashtray in the Linden home.

"The reason we came, Alan," said Joan, "is that Grandpa is worried. He wanted to come and talk to you, because you're just about the only person we know in Soda Creek, and he thought it best we tell someone."

Alan looked at Kelly, questioningly. She nodded, understanding what he was asking. "Yes, Dad. The same problem as Miss O. and the rest of us."

"Will you tell us about the little girl?" asked Alan. "Who saw her, and where was she?"

"Ah. You know already about the child. Is she safe?" Basil's voice was deep and rough, like gravel moving on the shallow bed of a stream.

"How did she get so far from home?" asked Joan.

"Too small to be out alone," said Basil. "Too small to be running away in the dark. I asked her, 'Hey, what are you doing here?' She put her hands out to me, like she wanted to be picked up. Then she started to cry, cry hard, but not making any noise. Then she went."

"I hope she's all right," said Joan. "Grandpa and I went and looked up and down the road for her, but then I started wondering if he was just seeing things, because no kid could have gone far in the dark and she wasn't anywhere near his cabin. I should have called you then, but I wasn't sure whether Grandpa. . ." Her voice trailed off, worried.

"Don't worry, Joan. She's safe." Basil and Joan waited patiently for Alan to go on. He looked at Kelly, wanting her to be the one to tell about the ghost. But Kelly wanted no part of the explanation. Telling people they had seen a ghost wasn't the easiest thing to do, and she had already done her share of explaining this morning. It was her father's turn.

"Go ahead, Dad," she said. "You tell them."

"Is there something wrong with the kid?" asked Joan, concerned. "Grandpa said she looked different, but he didn't explain how. That's when I decided he was making things up, and stopped worrying about her. She isn't retarded, is she?"

Alan sat silently, obviously not knowing how to begin to explain. David took pity on him and, taking Kelly's picture of the little ghost from the top of the fridge where he had placed it out of reach of the twins' sticky fingers, he handed it to Basil. "Is this the little girl you saw?" he asked.

Basil crunched out the stub of his cigarette, and reached for the picture. His fingers were gnarled and knotted, the knuckles as thick as chestnuts. He held the picture close to his face, studied it carefully, then passed it to Joan. "Yes," he said. "She is the one I saw in my cabin, early, before the sun came up."

Joan studied the picture, too. "Did you draw this, Kelly? It's good. But why did you put the child in those old fashioned clothes?"

"Because that's the way she was dressed, Chief . . . uh, Joan." answered Kelly. "That's what she wears when she appears to people."

"Appears? What is this? Are you making fun of us?" Joan looked from Alan to Kelly and back again, her eyes flashing, her long hair slapping against her cheeks as her head moved.

"You mean 'appears', like a ghost, a spirit," said Basil, nodding.

"Yes." Alan spoke quickly, trying to make them understand. "You're not the only one who has seen her, Basil. Kelly saw her, and David and others as well. It sounds weird, but we really think she is a ghost."

"Come on!" Joan still wasn't sure that she wasn't being made the brunt of a practical joke. "You can't expect us to believe that. She must live somewhere around here. She's white, so she sure doesn't live on the reserve."

"No," Kelly broke in, "no, she doesn't live anywhere around here Joan, honestly. There are only the twins here, and the kids are all older down at David's place."

Basil had taken the picture again, and was gently tracing the small face with one twisted finger. "Yes," he said. "A spirit, a *semec*. When I saw her, I wondered, but I am an old man. My eyes are tired. They're not good anymore. Last night, I wondered."

"Oh, come on Grandpa, don't start with that shaman stuff again!" Joan still looked annoyed, as if she would quite happily get up from the table and walk out of the house. "Grandpa's been teaching the old ways of our people, teaching everyone the dances and how to build a sweat lodge and use the cleansing smoke. That's fine, but now he figures he's got powers or something, like the medicine men, shamans, used to have."

Aware of Joan's irritation, Kelly quickly took the coffee from the stove. David, without being asked, had found clean mugs and set them on the table. "I know," he said to Joan. "I was upset myself when Kelly showed me that picture and told me I'd seen a ghost. I mean, that sort of thing just doesn't happen in this day and age."

Basil looked up at David. "The old ones, they knew about such things. To them it was not so hard to understand that sometimes spirits should want to come back to earth. There is a dance for the spirits. I taught it to the dancers yesterday. Maybe she heard our song and our drums, and that is why she came."

"Honestly, Grandpa, sometimes I wonder about you! There aren't any ghosts or spirits or whatever you want to call them, native or white. The old ways are gone for so many of our people; the old ways of living *and* the old ways of fighting. Now we have to fight through the Assembly of First Nations and land claims, not with dances and chants. You are teaching our people to spend so much time in the past that they forget to fight for their future."

Basil smiled at his granddaughter, reaching for his coffee. "I am an old man, Joan. I like to remember the old ways, and I want to teach them to others, so they will not be forgotten. But the old and the new, they can work together. We will do a warrior dance for you, when you go to that conference. Maybe the old can help the new." He grinned at Kelly's father. "Perhaps it is a good thing that the old ones did not let the women fight in battle. If the women all fought as fiercely as my granddaughter, perhaps there would be none of us left now!"

"Oh, Grandpa, you're impossible!" Joan's anger seemed to be forgotten, and she, too, smiled. "Go ahead, teach your dances and your legends. But I'm going to fight the modern way, use modern tools—the press, lawyers, road blocks. Wait until you see the recommendation I'm making at that conference."

"We will send you away with prayers and with the smell of sweetgrass in your hair, Joan. But for now we must find out more about the little white ghost."

"There's nothing more we can tell you," said Alan. "I wish there were. I guess we'll just have to wait for a while, wait and see if she comes back."

"Maybe she's finished visiting Soda Creek," said David. "Maybe it was just a one-shot appearance."

"Well, if other people have seen her too, then I guess she really is some sort of ghost," said Joan. "But I'm certainly not going to tell anyone else about it. They'd think we were all crazy."

"No. I don't think I'll talk about it either," said Kelly. "It isn't the sort of thing you bring up casually in the school cafeteria."

"Well," said Alan, pushing away his half empty coffee mug, "I have a feeling that she's done with us, that no one will see her again. Perhaps we'll find out that ghosts appeared all over the world last night, something to do with the stage of the moon or satellites or the weather. I'm going to forget all about her for now. I think she's gone."

"No." Old Basil's voice was firm. "She will be back. She has not done with us yet."

Everyone in the kitchen looked at him. He sat without moving, staring into space at something only he could see.

"I hope you're wrong, sir," said Kelly. "I hope she's gone for good. She made me feel so sad, just standing there, tears in her eyes. She was so little, so helpless. It was almost as if she were asking me to do something for her, but she didn't talk and I don't know what she wanted. I hope she's found whatever she was looking for, and is gone."

"Wait," said Basil. "Wait. You will see. She will be back, many times."

He spoke as if he were certain that the little ghost would return, and Kelly shivered slightly in the warm kitchen, glancing at the empty corner by the fridge to see if, in fact, the ghost had already returned and was standing there.

"Watch for her," said Basil. "Wait for her. She will be back."

Chapter 7

Kelly saw no ghost that Sunday night. She and her father had gone to Williams Lake for an early dinner. David, looking pale and drawn, had left shortly after Joan and Basil. "Time for my afternoon nap," he explained, trying to sound cheerful. "Some days I just seem to run down and have to spend time in bed. The doctor says I'm over the worst, and I'm not even contagious anymore, but my body won't listen." He smiled at Kelly as he left, and once again she noticed how his smile transformed his face. "See you tomorrow, Kelly," he said. "If that's okay?"

The dinner had been good, steak and lobster tails, baked potato with sour cream and fluffy chocolate cheesecake for dessert. Over dinner Kelly and her father talked, sitting a long time after the meal was finished. "Well, it isn't breakfast, and we aren't in Soda Creek, but I feel as if we've had some time together, the way we used to," said Alan. "You're right, you know, Kelly. I haven't had much time for you lately. I'm sorry."

"It's all right, Dad. I was just upset at Miss O. this morning. You don't have to take me out for dinner every Sunday. And, if our little ghost-child has finished visiting us, I shouldn't be that upset again for a while."

"If she's gone," said her father. "Basil seemed sure that we haven't seen the last of her." Somehow, the mention of the ghost ended their talking, and they drove home to Soda Creek in silence.

"Good night, Kelly. Sleep well, little one. No ghostly visitors tonight, I hope," said Alan as Kelly headed for bed.

"I hope not, Dad. I'm exhausted. See you in the morning."

The next morning, however, Kelly's father was unusually quiet. Even the radio was silent, as Alan moved around the kitchen, making lunches. He muttered something that could have been 'good morning' and finished wrapping sandwiches.

"Sleep well, Dad?"

"Fine. Eat your breakfast." And that was all he said. Kelly was concerned. Normally her father was a cheerful riser, punctuating his morning chores with whistles and comments to the radio show host, talking to Kelly. This morning the sound of Kelly swallowing orange juice sounded loud in the kitchen.

"Dad? You okay? You didn't come down with David's mono overnight, did you?"

"No." Her father was brusque, and he snapped his lunch pail closed with more force than necessary. "You heard him say that he's not contagious."

Kelly, still wondering what was wrong, kept talking. "Hey, I didn't have any visitations last night. Maybe the ghost has finished with Soda Creek, in spite of what Basil thinks."

"I don't want to talk about it this morning." Alan's voice was sharp, and he left the kitchen abruptly, lunch box in hand. "See you this evening, Kelly. I'll get the shopping."

"What is wrong with Dad?" wondered Kelly. It wasn't at all like her father to be so taciturn. Then she knew. She may not have seen the little ghost last night, but somehow she knew that her father had, and that was what was upsetting him. It was one thing for him to listen to other people's stories of seeing a ghost-child, but much more difficult for her father to accept seeing it himself. Perhaps, in spite of all his reassurances to the others who had seen her, he still believed that the ghost had been their personal apparition, something Alan would never have to face himself.

"Poor Dad," Kelly thought. "In spite of everyone who told him about seeing the ghost yesterday, he didn't really believe it. No wonder he's upset."

She finished her juice, still thinking about her father. Well, she wouldn't pressure him to tell her about it. When her father was ready, he would share his experience with her. Kelly remembered how she had felt early Sunday morning, how upset and confused *she* had been when she saw the ghost.

Breakfast finished, her own lunch packed, and the dishes stacked, ready to wash when she got home from school, Kelly headed out the door for the short walk to the school bus stop. Every morning the bus made the winding trip down the gravel road from the highway to pick up Kelly, the twins, four students from the commune and half a dozen children from the reserve. This morning the twins were sitting on the garden fence, waiting for her, their coats open in spite of the December cold.

"Hi, guys," she said. "Do up your jackets, you'll freeze."

"Hi, Kelly," answered Trisha. Tommy just nodded, and fell into step beside her as they headed up the road.

"Tommy's sulky this morning," said Trisha, obediently tugging at the zipper on her jacket.

Kelly looked at the boy trudging along beside her, his head bowed, his eyes firmly on the ground. He, too, had done up his jacket without being told a second time, Kelly noticed, surprised. "Troubles, Tommy?" she asked.

"No," said Tommy, then he fell silent again.

Trisha, however, was anything but silent, talking incessantly all the way to the bus stop, about her gym class, her new running shoes, Tommy being in trouble for being grouchy this morning, and the video movie her father had promised to bring home that night. Tommy didn't once contradict her, correct her, or even interrupt her.

"Something strange is going on," Kelly thought. Then, as clearly as she had known about her father, she knew that Tommy, too, had seen the little ghost last night.

Trisha ran ahead to the bus stop, but Tommy stayed with Kelly. "What's with you this morning, Tommy?" she asked.

"Nothing." Tommy's voice was low. He looked around him as if to make sure that no one could hear him, then asked, "Hey, do you really think that little girl is a ghost?"

"I guess so, Tommy. There doesn't seem to be any other explanation, does there?"

"She doesn't look like a . . . never mind." His head

went down again, and he stayed silent until the bus pulled up.

"I'm right," Kelly thought. "He's seen her too, but he doesn't want to admit it, not after all the arguing he did with Trisha yesterday. Poor Tommy, finding out that ghosts aren't so 'dumb'. And poor Dad too. The whole idea does take some getting used to."

School drifted by that morning, slightly out of focus, blurred and not quite real. Kelly couldn't seem to keep her mind on what she was doing and found that she had copied the same algebra question twice, but got two different answers. Firmly she pulled her thoughts away from the tiny figure that was causing the inhabitants of Soda Creek so much anguish, and tried to concentrate on what was going on in the classroom.

As she headed for the cafeteria at lunch, Miss Overton approached her. "Kelly," she said, "Could I speak to you for a minute?"

The rest of the group Kelly usually ate with looked at her questioningly, then went on without her. Kelly hoped someone would save her a seat.

Miss Overton took Kelly's arm and urged her into the empty counsellor's office. "I'm SO sorry to take you away from your friends, Kelly," she said, her charm bracelet jangling as she shut the door, "but I DID want to talk to you, just for a moment."

"Okay." Kelly stood, waiting, a bit uncomfortable, remembering how rude she'd been to the teacher yesterday morning.

"I know you are a very RESPONSIBLE girl, Kelly, and very UNDERSTANDING, although you did have a bit of a temper tantrum yesterday. I just wanted to say . . . well, to ask you . . . I mean. . ." She gestured as she struggled for the right words, and Kelly wished she'd get on with what she was trying to say. She'd never get time to eat her lunch if Miss O. kept her too long.

"I just wanted to say, you know, it wouldn't be good for my REPUTATION, for my discipline with the students, if you told everyone I was seeing SUPERNATURAL beings." She looked pleadingly at Kelly. "You won't . . . I mean, you haven't told any of your friends, have you?"

Kelly suddenly felt almost sorry for the woman. "Of course," she thought. "Miss O. went to church yesterday morning after she left our place, and no one's told her that she wasn't the only one to see the ghost."

"It's okay, Miss O.," she said. "I haven't told anyone about the ghost you saw. And you weren't the only one to see it, you know. I saw her, and David from the commune, and Trisha, and I think my father saw her last night, although he hasn't come right out and said so. It's not just you. Something strange really is happening in Soda Creek."

Miss Overton collapsed into the chair behind the counsellor's desk. "You saw it, too?" she asked. "And other people. You mean, it really was a ghost?"

"We think she had to be," said Kelly. "but that's kind of hard to accept, isn't it? I mean, you can't go around telling people without having them think that you were a bit crazy."

"Oh, I am so RELIEVED!" Miss Overton waved her arms around her head, as if she were brushing away all her fears for her own sanity. "Oh, Kelly, I was so very CONCERNED yesterday. It just seemed so impossible that I thought that maybe I was. . ."

"I know," said Kelly. "That's the way we all feel.

But don't worry, Miss O. If you are going crazy, then half of Soda Creek is too."

"Oh, that's such a RELIEF. But I musn't take up any more of your lunch hour, Kelly. And I do thank you for sharing this with me."

"Sure. I should have told you yesterday. Sorry."

"Well, we all have our IRRATIONAL moments, don't we? But I did have such a comforting talk with my priest after the service yesterday."

However, shortly after lunch, Kelly realized that Miss O., reassured by the fact that ghost-sighting was epidemic in Soda Creek, must have spent her lunch hour elaborating on the story. Kelly's first afternoon class was English, and her teacher looked at her strangely.

"Been reading Hamlet lately, Kelly? I hear you've been seeing apparitions on your own castle walls, you and the others at Soda Creek. Better get your water supply tested. Probably something hallucinogenic in it."

Kelly was furious. "Isn't that just like Miss O.," she thought. "One moment she's begging me not to tell anyone about the ghost, and then five minutes later she's entertaining the rest of the teachers with stories of the Soda Creek 'haunting'."

Kelly was still in a bad mood when she got off the school bus that afternoon. The story of the little ghost had spread through the school, and her friends had begun to question her, disbelieving. When she walked into her last class of the day, there was a hastily drawn chalk ghost on the blackboard with the words, "Look, Kelly, look. See the ghost. Run, Kelly, run." Now that everyone in the high school seemed to know about the ghost, it wouldn't be long before word reached all of

Williams Lake, which was still a small enough town to enjoy spreading a good story.

"I guess I'm still thinking of her as 'my' ghost," she thought. "It's almost as if I don't want to share her with anyone, especially anyone outside of Soda Creek."

Her mood lightened, though, when she saw David waiting for her. He was carrying a brown paper bag, and he looked a lot stronger than he had when he left yesterday afternoon.

"Hi," she called. "Enjoy your nap yesterday?"

"Sure did. I slept for three hours. That doesn't happen much anymore, but I think I spent all of October in bed."

"Want to come in?" Kelly asked, opening the front door.

"Well, I've got stewing beef here and some vegetables from the root cellar, and if you let me in I might let you sample 'Stanton's Special Stew'."

"Inviting yourself for dinner, are you?"

"Why not? I figure it will be edible if I can keep you out of the kitchen."

Kelly whirled on him, her earlier irritation returning. "Listen, I'm getting fed up with jokes about my cooking. It's not too bad when Dad does it, but you haven't eaten anything I've cooked except bacon. Drop it, will you?"

"Sorry." David took the bag of groceries to the kitchen, Kelly following him. "Sorry," he said again, and put a hand on her shoulder. "I was just kidding. I didn't know you were really sensitive about it. You see, I figured if I offered to cook supper, then you would let me stay and eat with you. It was just a way of getting myself invited."

"It's okay," said Kelly, no longer cross. "I'm kind of upset right now." And as she washed the breakfast dishes, and David browned the meat and started it simmering, she told him about her day; about her father's unexplained moodiness in the morning, Tommy's sullenness, and about Clara Overton spreading the story of the little ghost, once she realized that she had not been the only person to be 'haunted'.

"And then there was that dumb ghost on the blackboard, and the snide comments from my friends. It hasn't been a good day. And by now most of Williams Lake knows about our ghost. They'll probably even put it in the paper!"

"That might not be such a bad thing," commented David. "Maybe someone will be able to help get rid of her."

Kelly put the last dish away, and sighed. "That's it; I guess. I don't want to get rid of her. At least, I don't want her to go away as unhappy as she is."

There was silence in the kitchen while David began to peel a large onion. "I know what you mean," he said finally. "My aunt saw her last night. Asked me all sorts of questions about the little girl I'd seen in the barn, and then finally admitted that she'd seen her too. She wasn't frightened by the little thing, just worried about her."

"Little thing, little one," said Kelly absently, and her eyes began to water. Must be the onion David was slicing, she thought, brushing at her eyes. "But David, we have to do something about her. No one will get any sleep if she keeps on visiting us every night. Poor little one."

"Hey!" David quickly threw the onion into the pot, adjusting the heat under it. "Hey," he said again, moving to stand beside her. "You're not crying, are you?"

"No. It must be the onion. And I am worried, David. What are we going to do?" Strange, she thought. The onion was safely in the stew, she could hardly smell it anymore, yet her eyes still stung.

"I know what I'm going to do," said David. He moved behind Kelly, and slipped off the ribbon that she had tied around her forehead that morning.

"What. . ." she said, startled.

His fingers began to loosen the rubber bands that held her French braids. "I want to see what that hair of yours looks like when it isn't braided up, the way you wear it all the time."

"David! Leave it alone. I look awful with my hair down."

"Nope. You can braid it again, it's all coming out and untidy, anyway." His fingers gently separated the strands, untangling her thick hair, smoothing it as it fell past her shoulders.

Kelly stood still, unable to move. Her mother . . . her mother was the last one who had touched her hair that way, gently untangling it, talking to Kelly as she brushed it. Even at thirteen Kelly's mother had still done her hair for her every morning. Since her mother's death, Kelly had let her hair grow, not bothering with it, twisting it roughly into braids or a pony tail, never getting it cut, or even trimmed. It had been nearly three years since her mother. . .

"Don't," she said, once again near tears, hearing her mother's voice as the brush would pull through her tangled hair. "Ah, Kelly, little one, what are we going to do with this hair of yours?"

David put both hands on her shoulders, turning her to face him. Kelly's hands flew to her head, pulling her hair back, flattening it against her ears. "It looks awful," she said.

"No, it doesn't," David said, softly. "It looks magnificent. Wild, untamed, like a jungle animal—or a goddess." His hands slid to her face, cupping her cheeks, while his fingers tangled themselves in her hair.

"Always had a thing for redheads," he said, and bent to kiss her.

Neither of them heard the front door fly open, or the hurrying footsteps that tore through the house, into the kitchen.

"Look, he's kissing Kelly!"

"That is so dumb!" The Terpen twins had arrived.

David stepped away from Kelly, and she stood there, flustered. "Ever hear of ringing a doorbell or knocking?" she asked. "And go back right now and take those boots off."

"But, Kelly. . ."

"You have to come, quick."

"Hurry, come right now."

"At Mr. Crinchley's house. There's noises. . ."

"Yeah, at the Grinch's."

"Sort of moaning and crying."

"Someone keeps saying over and over. . ."

"A ghost, a ghost. . ."

"A ghost!"

Chapter 8

Almost before the twins had paused to take a breath, David was out the door, running down the street towards Ed Crinchley's house. Kelly stopped to pull on her coat, then she, too, flew out of the house, followed closely by the excited twins.

"It's a real scary voice, Kelly."

"And it says, 'a ghost, a ghost,' just like that."

"Wait for us, Kelly."

"Maybe it's got old Grinch."

The door to the old man's house stood open, and David was nowhere to be seen. Since the inhabitants of Soda Creek seldom locked their homes, it wasn't surprising that David had been able to enter. Rather nervously, Kelly climbed the stairs, the twins right behind her, and stepped through the open door. "David?" she called, then coughed. Miss O. was right, Ed Crinchley's house did smell funny. Almost like something rotting.

"David!" she called again, afraid to go any further

into the gloomy house until she heard his voice. Trisha moved closer and reached for Kelly's hand, while Tommy took a step backwards, as if he were having second thoughts about being in the 'ghost' house.

"Kelly, quickly. Down the stairs, in the basement," called David.

Kelly took a deep breath and walked into the dark hallway. Halfway along, dim light spilled from a partly open door, and David's voice came from that doorway.

"Get some water, Kelly, and bring it down. He's hurt."

"I can get the water," said Trisha. "I can find the kitchen."

"Go with her, Tommy," Kelly said to the reluctant boy. "Hurry. I'm going to see what's happened."

The partly open door led to the basement of the house, the steps down to it were narrow and steep, painted a dull red. As Kelly moved cautiously down the stairs, the peculiar smell got stronger, much stronger. "David?" she said, and then she saw them.

Ed Crinchley sat propped up against a wall, underneath a dirt-grimed window, his face white and creased with pain. One of his pant legs had been rolled up, and David was inspecting his ankle.

"Leave the blasted thing alone and get me upstairs," the old man growled. "What took you so long? I've been lying here for hours."

"Are you all right, Mr. Crinchley?" asked Kelly.

"Of course I'm not! I've gone and hurt my ankle and knocked over a whole five gallon jug of crabapple wine. One of my best batches, too."

Kelly suddenly realized what the strange smell was; home-made wine, fermenting, brewing, or whatever it was that fruit and yeast did to turn into wine.

"He says he came down to bottle some wine, slipped on the stairs and rolled half-way across the basement," said David. He sat back on his heels, facing the old man. "I think it's broken," he said. "We'll have to get you to a hospital."

"No way I'm going to that place," snarled Ed Crinchley. "Blasted hospitals." He glared at Tommy and Trisha as they came down the stairs, the glass of water in Trisha's hand dripping.

"What happened, Mr. Crinchley?"

"Here's some water. Tommy found the glass." Trisha handed the old man the water, and he drank noisily.

"What's the matter with you kids?" he asked. "I heard you outside when you got off the school bus, shouted my fool head off. What took you so long to get help?"

"Was it you shouting?"

"We thought it was the ghost."

The glass fell from Ed Crinchley's hand. "Who said I saw a ghost?" he demanded. "Never did, never. Don't believe in the little critters, anyway."

At the word 'little' Kelly and David looked at each other. Kelly knelt down beside the hurt man and put a hand on his shoulder. "It's all right," she said. "We've seen her, too. She really is a ghost."

"Did she visit you, too?" asked Tommy.

"Was she looking for your bathroom? I don't think you have a bathroom down here, just all these bottles and junk." Trisha wrinkled her nose as she looked around the cluttered basement.

"Never mind right now, twins," said David. "Run home and ask your mother to bring her car and some blankets, as fast as she can. Mr. Crinchley's hurt, he has to go to hospital."

As reluctant to leave as they had been to enter the house, the twins started slowly up the stairs. "Hurry!" David urged. "Go on, run!"

Ed Crinchley slumped against the wall, his head dropping to his chest. David took his wrist, feeling for his pulse. "He's okay," he said, "but I think he's in more pain than he's letting on. We've got to get him some help as soon as we can."

"A ghost. . ." The old man stirred, his lips trembling as a moan escaped them. "A ghost. . ."

Kelly jumped. "Is he asleep, David?"

"No, I think he's blacked out, probably from the pain and the shock. I guess he's been doing that all afternoon, moving in and out of consciousness, moaning like that. He was quite alert when I first got here, and he said it was just after noon when he came down to work on this wine."

"That's what the twins heard, then," said Kelly, and she patted the unconscious man's shoulder gently. "Poor man. Lying here all alone, hurting, and wondering if he really had seen a ghost. Will he be all right, David?"

"Hey, I'm not a doctor, I've only had some first aid training. I think he'll be okay if we can keep him warm and get him to the hospital soon. I guess it's lucky he doesn't have a heart condition, or the shock could have killed him."

"The ghost must have been near the stairs," said Kelly. "There's not much light down here, so he saw her in the gloom. He wouldn't have been frightened if he could have seen her properly."

Footsteps clattered down the stairs as the twins returned. "Mom's here with the car."

"She says you can drive him to the hospital, she can't leave us alone."

"Yeah. We want to come too, but she won't let us."

David slipped his hands under Ed Crinchley's shoulders. "Help me, Kelly. I think we can manage. He's very thin, hardly weighs anything." Carefully, gently, they lifted the old man and inched their way up the stairs. He stayed only half conscious, muttering about the ghost and his spilled crabapple wine, as they eased him into the Terpen's station wagon.

"Oh, Kelly, hurry. I'll phone the hospital and tell them you're coming." The twins' mother covered the unconscious man with a blanket, tucking it firmly around him. "Hurry," she said again. "The keys are in the ignition, and there's lots of gas."

Kelly slid into the driver's seat and started the engine. "Thanks, Mrs. Terpen. Phone the R.C.M.P. too, and see if there's a patrol car near here. Maybe they could lead us in—it would be faster."

As she pulled away, Kelly rolled down her window and shouted, "The stew, Mrs. Terpen, on the stove. . ." She saw the woman nod, and hoped she had understood, that she would go to Kelly's house and turn off the heat under the stew.

A few miles later as they neared the end of the steep gravel road, close to where it joined Highway 97, they heard the whine of a siren. Their police escort had arrived.

* * * * *

It was after six when Kelly and David finally left the hospital in Williams Lake, and headed back up the dark highway towards Soda Creek. David had offered to drive home, and Kelly sat beside him, her head back against the headrest, exhausted. It had begun to snow, not heavily, just a sprinkling of small flakes. As the car moved forward, the snow, caught in the headlights, seemed to whirl towards the windshield like a million tiny falling stars. Kelly watched the snow, too tired to speak. Ed Crinchley's ankle was badly sprained; it had been securely taped and the old man was resting quietly, heavily sedated.

"Those nurses are in for quite a time of it when he wakes up," Kelly said at last. "I don't think he cares for hospitals, and he'll be sure everyone around him knows it!"

"I'm beginning to see why he's called 'the Grinch'," said David. "He's tough, all right, and a good thing too, or he'd be in a lot worse shape than he is."

"I guess so," answered Kelly, yawning and rubbing her forehead as she did. Suddenly she sat upright, now wide awake. "My hair!" she said. "It's been down all this time. Why didn't you tell me? It's a mess."

David looked away from the road for a moment, then turned back, grinning. "Well," he said. "That mane of yours certainly has a mind of its own. It's almost standing straight out from your head."

"Thanks a lot," Kelly snapped. "Weren't you the one who said something about the hair of a goddess a while ago?" Then she blushed, turning to look out the side window so David couldn't see her face, as the memory of those few moments in the kitchen came back to her. The tension of the last hours, including a high-speed trip to the hospital following a police car with its lights flashing and siren screaming, had driven the thought of David's kiss out of her mind. Until now.

"Goddess?" I must have been thinking of the one who lives on a rock in the ocean. You know, Medusa. The one with snakes growing out of her head instead of hair."

"David Stanton, that's not fair. Can't you ever be serious? Do you have to joke about everything?" Kelly kept her face turned away from him, not wanting him to see her eyes. Something inside her had turned softly over when she remembered the incident in the kitchen, and she had felt her face go red. Why should she react this way after just one kiss, she wondered? She meant nothing to David, she was just someone to spend time with while he was in Soda Creek, away from university, away from his friends, maybe even away from someone else, someone very important in his life. "Some of your jokes aren't very funny," she said in a small voice, then repeated. "Can't you ever be serious?"

"But I am serious." David reached over and took her hand, holding it firmly in his. "Very, very serious, my little Kelly."

Chapter 9

From the windows of the Soda Creek homes light splashed across the dark road, welcoming, warm. David pulled up outside the Linden home and said, "I'll take the car back to Mrs. Terpen. And then I'd better check in with Uncle George. Maybe I'll see you later?"

"I guess so," Kelly answered, still feeling awkward. "You never did finish making your 'special' stew. Let's hope Dad figured out what was for dinner, and threw in the rest of the vegetables. I'll save you some, if you like."

Alan came out and stood on the front porch as Kelly watched David drive the short distance down the road to the Terpen house. "How is Ed, Kelly?" he asked. "The twins were waiting for me, talking so quickly that I could barely understand them, and Mrs. Terpen left me a note saying where you were. Ben cleaned up all the spilled wine in Ed's basement. What happened, anyway? Is Ed okay?"

Inside, the house was full of the smell of stew, and Kelly realized she was very hungry. "Mr. Crinchley's got a bad sprain, Dad, but he'll be okay. It was the little ghost again. He saw her in his basement, and fell down the stairs. He'll be using crutches for a while, and I'll bet this accident hasn't helped his temper any, but he'll be fine."

"That could have been serious, Kelly. It seems as if the little ghost isn't quite as harmless as we think."

"Oh, Dad, she doesn't mean to scare anyone. She just startled the Grinch. It's not serious."

"I wonder," said Alan, then changed the subject. "Come on, let's get some food inside you, then we'll worry about the ghost. Looks like a good stew you started. I didn't know we had any stewing beef left in the freezer."

"David brought it," said Kelly. "He was making stew when the twins arrived to tell us about the Grinch."

"Yes." Her father's face was serious. "Yes. The twins did say that David was here. They were quite clear when they told me about that—and about what the two of you were doing."

"Come on, Dad, it's nothing to get upset about." Kelly knew she was blushing again, and she turned away.

"Perhaps not, Kelly, but I was surprised. You've only known David a day and. . ." Her father's voice trailed off as he searched for the right words.

"It's all right, Dad. I can look after myself. And I am sixteen. Anyway, can we please eat and not talk about it right now?"

Her father spooned out a bowl of the stew. It was

thick and hot, but before Kelly could take a bite, the doorbell rang.

"I'll get it," said Alan. "Eat your dinner, Kelly. You look as if you need something nourishing."

"I *don't* need any company right now," thought Kelly. "I don't even want to see David again until I've eaten and fixed my hair."

But it wasn't David at the door. Kelly could hear that only too clearly as a woman's voice filtered down to the kitchen.

"But really, Alan, we can't let this sort of thing go on happening. It MUST be stopped." Clara Overton swept into the kitchen, flinging an arm around Kelly, her charm bracelet jangling. "Oh, my dear, how BRAVE you were. To go into that awful house, so UNSANITARY, and take that poor old man to hospital."

"Not really. . ." Kelly began, pulling away from the woman's embrace.

"Oh, yes, and that nice David, too, so COMPETENT. Mrs. Terpen says he's quite good looking." She looked at Kelly coyly, smiling knowingly.

"Those rotten twins!" thought Kelly. Obviously Tommy and Trisha had spread the story of David kissing her to everyone in Soda Creek.

"But, as I was saying to your father, this can NOT go on! That horrible little ghost thing can't keep on jumping out in front of people, scaring them half to DEATH! We simply can not allow her to stay here any longer."

"Um, sure, Miss O., that's a great idea, but just how are we going to get her to leave? And besides," Kelly went on, more softly, "besides, she didn't mean to hurt Mr. Crinchley. It's not her fault that people are frightened of her."

"I have a PLAN, Kelly, and your father agrees that it just might work."

Kelly looked at her father, who busied himself at the stove, refusing to meet her eyes.

"A PRIEST," Miss Overton announced triumphantly. "A priest to exorcise the ghost and send her away forever!"

"What? But you can't do that to her. She's not an evil spirit that needs to be exorcised, a demon or something wicked, Miss O. She's just lost and. . ."

"Easy, Kelly." Alan moved beside Kelly, one hand on her shoulder. "Clara doesn't mean a real exorcism, that takes months to get approved. She just wants her own priest to come out here and say a few prayers."

"But we can't send the ghost away until we know what she wants and why she's here!" Kelly was angry now, her dinner pushed to one side, her hands clenched. "Please, don't send her away yet."

"But we can't have her popping up at all hours of the day and night, frightening people, Kelly. Especially not when her appearance results in someone getting hurt, as happened to Ed today. Next time it could be more serious."

Kelly sighed and unclenched her fists. "I know," she said softly, remembering Ed Crinchley's pale face, the pain lines slashing deeply across it, and the way he'd kept fading in and out of consciousness. "I know. But I don't want her hurt."

"You can't HURT a ghost, Kelly." Miss Overton had been listening to the exchange between Kelly and her father with a puzzled expression on her face. "And you can't keep a ghost around the way you'd keep a stray KITTEN. I don't understand you, Kelly."

"You're right, Miss O. I just don't seem to be able to think rationally about her. She seemed so. . ."

"Perhaps it's your age, Kelly. Girls your age tend to be ROMANTICISTS about everything."

"Maybe."

"Anyway, it's all arranged. Father Glenn will be here at eight—why that's less than an hour from now. You will come, won't you Kelly? I've just got time to pop some rhubarb muffins in the oven, and I'll make fresh coffee for us all."

"What?" Kelly was confused.

"Clara wants us to go over to her house this evening, Kelly, and talk to the priest," explained Alan.

"Tonight? You mean he's coming here tonight, Dad?" There was a shrillness in Kelly's voice that surprised her.

"Yes. It will be okay, Kelly. It can't hurt, you know."

"No," said Kelly. "It can't hurt *us* anyway."

"See you later, then," Miss Overton called, heading for the door. She was drawn back to the kitchen by Alan's voice.

"Clara? Do we need to have all the people who have seen the ghost present for this—for whatever the priest will do—to work?"

"I don't know, Alan. But we'll have an evening together, you and me and Kelly. And Father Glenn."

Alan grinned at his daughter, then turned back to the teacher. "Really, Clara, I think the whole community should be invited to participate in this. We should invite the others who have seen the ghost as well."

"Others? Oh, yes, Kelly did say that other people had . . . of course, Alan, if you think. . ." Miss Overton seemed flustered.

"Definitely, Clara. We should all be there. I'll tell Ben, and perhaps you'd phone the Terpens and see if the twins can join us, too."

"Ben? One of the men who live in the house with the big garden?"

"Sure, Clara. Ben saw the ghost just after you did. You must invite him."

Miss Overton seemed very uneasy. "Yes, well, I mean, I've NEVER had one of them in my house before."

"And David," said Kelly. "He saw the ghost, too."

"Well, yes, certainly do invite your friend, Kelly. Such a nice young man. I'll make extra muffins, but I really don't know if the twins. . ." She hurried away, muttering to herself.

"Dad! That was cruel," said Kelly. "I think Miss O. was planning a quiet evening with us, especially you."

"Well, at least I didn't tell her that Basil had seen the ghost too, and insist that she invite him and Joan."

"No." Kelly was silent for a moment, thinking of her own reaction when Joan and Basil had arrived at the door yesterday morning. "No. I don't think Miss O. is ready for that yet."

"Well, eat up, Kelly, and let's get these dishes done and those invitations to Clara's 'ghostbusting' party issued."

And when Kelly and her father arrived, somewhat late, at Miss Overton's home, there was a sense of a party in the air. Father Glenn, a tall young man with a full, black beard, sat in a big armchair, Tommy and Trisha at his feet. On the coffee table was a jumble of canvas and bright strands of wool, and Bob and Clara sat shuffling through patterns. "I had no IDEA you were interested in this kind of work," Kelly heard the teacher say as she and her father let themselves in. "You must bring more of your projects and let me see them, Bob. How nice to find someone who shares my interest in the CREATIVE crafts."

Ben was pouring coffee from a large coffee butler on the dining room table, and he greeted them with a smile. "Hi. Bob brought Clara one of his crewel pieces, and the two of them have been buried in that pile of wool ever since. And the twins have been keeping Father Glenn well entertained."

"Oh, Kelly, Alan, you're here. And you too, David," said Miss Overton as the door opened again and David looked in.

"Hi. I knocked but no one seemed to hear me," he said.

"Come in. Here, let me take your coats. Father Glenn, this is Kelly and Alan Linden and David." The teacher was flushed with excitement, and her arms flew as she spoke, gesturing. "My, I had no idea this would be such FUN."

"Yes, Clara," said the young priest, "but time is moving on, and I heard you promise Mrs. Terpen that the twins wouldn't be out too late on a school night. Maybe we should get to work on your problem."

"Problem?" asked Trisha.

"He means the ghost, stupid," answered her brother.

"Ghosts aren't problems. They're just . . . just ghosts!"

"Tommy and Trisha have been telling me about how they saw the ghost, and Clara has told me of her sighting," said the priest. "If the rest of you would share your experiences, it would give me a better idea of the scale of the problem. And perhaps some clue as to what would be the best thing to do."

Everyone settled down and, somewhat reluctantly, the other sightings were reported. Alan looked apologetically at his daughter, aware that he hadn't told her directly that he, too, had seen the little ghost. Then he told of meeting the small girl in his still dark hallway early in the morning as he went to the kitchen to start preparing breakfast. David told of the ghost's visit to the cow barn, and Ben explained how he had seen her out in his garden, near the raspberry canes.

"My aunt has seen her, too," added David.

"And Basil from the reserve," said Alan.

"From the RESERVE?" Miss Overton's voice was shrill. "Oh, I had no idea that they. . ."

"I suppose there's still time to phone and invite Basil and Joan," said Kelly, her face straight.

"Oh, do you think I should?"

"It's all right, Clara," said Alan, coming to her rescue. "You have a large enough houseful for tonight. I'm sure Basil will forgive you for not inviting him."

Father Glenn cleared his throat. "When Clara asked me to come out here," he said, "I didn't know what to say to her. I didn't realize that so many of you had seen this little ghost, so many different people. And dealing with ghosts is something I've never had to do before."

"Can't you do nothing, then?" asked Tommy.

"You mean, she'll just have to stay?" added Trisha.

The twins had been surprisingly quiet for a while, but now showed every sign of making up for that silence.

"In *Ghostbusters* they had this electronic thing," said Trisha.

"Yeah. With coloured lines coming out from it."

"It was real scary."

"Was not. You're a chicken, Trish."

"Am not!"

"Hold it, twins." The young priest spoke firmly. "I didn't say there wasn't anything I could do, just that I had never run into this problem before. I have come up with something that I think will help. I don't guarantee anything, but I don't think what I have in mind will hurt to try."

"Have you got one of those electronic things, too?"

"Can I try it? Please?" Tommy's eyes were wide at the thought of actually getting his hands on a 'ghost-busting' machine.

"It's not that exciting, Tommy. Sorry. Just some prayers, and some special water we use in our church. Holy water. I brought quite a bit of it, not knowing how much we'd need." He reached down beside his chair and brought up an ice-cream bucket, firmly lidded, half full of water.

"It looks ordinary to me," said Tommy, disappointed. Around the room Kelly could see a few nods as some of the adults silently agreed with him.

"Yes, but this water has been blessed, so it isn't ordinary anymore, Tommy. When we bless the water we say special prayers over it, and I thought that I would say some of those prayers again, right here. Then we'll go to everyone's house and sprinkle this water around their doorways. Maybe that will keep your little ghost from pestering you."

"Oh, yes, Father. Do let's begin and put an end to all this FEAR," Miss Overton urged.

"I shall, Clara. That is, if all of you are in agreement

that this is what you wish?" No one answered him, but again heads nodded. The priest stood and took a purple stole from his pocket. He kissed it, then draped it around his neck. The room grew quiet, all eyes on him, expectantly. He crossed himself, and began.

"Oh, water, creature of God, may you put to flight and drive away from the places where you are sprinkled every apparition, villainy, and turn of devilish deceit, and every unclean spirit." He paused, crossed himself again, and continued. "Every unclean spirit. Almighty and everlasting God, bless this water which you created and gave to the use of mankind, so that it may rid whatever it touches or sprinkles of all uncleanliness and protect it from every assault of evil spirits. Let whatever might menace the safety of those who live here be put to flight by the sprinkling of this water, so that all may be secure against all attack. Amen."

There was silence for a moment, and then Tommy spoke.

"Is that all?"

"I thought it would be longer," said Trisha. "And more interesting."

Miss Overton gasped at the twins' comments, but Father Glenn smiled at the children. "That's all," he said. "It's just a small part of the special prayers for blessing the water. Since this water has already been blessed, I didn't think we'd need to do all the prayers over again. I can say more, make it longer, if you want."

"No," chorused the twins. "Can we go put water on the houses now?"

"Yes, of course," the priest answered, and the rest of the small congregation, assured that the blessing had finished, began to stand, reach for coats, hats and scarves, ready to follow Father Glenn out into the night. Ready to disinfect their small community, cleanse it of a ghost-child.

Tommy and Trisha were out the door first, urging the priest, now carefully holding the uncovered bucket of holy water, to hurry, hurry.

The twins stepped out the door first, but Kelly heard it first. "Listen!" she said. "Oh, listen to her."

Faintly, from somewhere, yet from nowhere in the December dark, a small, high sound came drifting down the snow-covered road, a sound as thin and unsubstantial as the smoke from a chimney, yet just as real. The sound of crying. The heart wrenching sound of a small child crying and crying and crying.

Chapter 10

"Leave her alone, leave her alone!" Kelly's voice rose above the thin sound of crying. She reached out, tore the bucket of holy water from the astonished priest's hand, and threw it across Clara Overton's snow-covered lawn. "Can't you hear? She's frightened, hurting. Don't chase her away, leave her alone!"

A gust of wind caught the empty bucket, rolling it gently across the crisp snow, making a scraping noise that seemed loud in the sudden stillness. The crying had stopped.

Kelly spoke softly into the silence. "It's all right now, little one. It's all right." Then she burst into tears herself.

"Kelly!" Alan Linden pushed his way through the silent crowd on the front porch, trying to reach his daughter, but Kelly was gone, running, still weeping, towards her own home. A door slammed, and once again there was silence.

"This is most upsetting," said Father Glenn. "I didn't really expect to experience your little ghost myself. I somehow thought—well, she has proved that she does exist."

"I'm sorry, Father. Kelly has developed a very strong attachment for the ghost-child. She hasn't been herself since she first saw her," apologized Alan.

"Kelly's in real trouble now, I bet." Tommy spoke almost cheerfully.

"Are you going to ground her, Mr. Linden?"

"We'd get a licking if we shouted at grown-ups the way Kelly did."

"Yeah. And grabbed things like that."

The twins' chatter seemed to prompt the adults, and they, too began to speak together. "Will Kelly be all right, Alan?" asked Bob, his gentle voice scarcely audible over Clara Overton's loud apology to Father Glenn for that "unseemly outburst of juvenile TEMPER," and the priest's assurances that neither he, nor the Church, had been offended.

"I understand better now," he said, "and I am the one who should be sorry. I had no idea that your ghost was so real, so real yet so troubled. I am afraid I have meddled where I shouldn't have."

Clara's guests told her good-bye, and made their way down the stairs, across the snow-covered lawn where a sheen of new ice crystals was all that was left of the holy water. Then, silent once again, they separated, heading for their own homes.

David fell into step beside Alan, who shook his head, explaining, "I'd rather you didn't come over right now, David. I think it would be better if I spoke with Kelly alone. I don't know why she is reacting this way."

"All right, Mr. Linden. I understand," said David, and turned around, taking a few steps down the road towards the commune at the far end. Then he hesitated and turned back, calling, "Is it all right, I mean, do you mind if I drop by tomorrow after school to see Kelly?"

Alan stood still, and for a moment it seemed as if he wasn't going to answer. Then he said, "Yes, I suppose you may, David. But remember that Kelly's very young. And very vulnerable right now."

"I understand, sir."

Ben and Bob had started down the road when Ben called to the priest who was unlocking the door of his small car. "Father, we seem to have abandoned you."

"You must think us a very inhospitable group," added Bob. "No one has thanked you for your trouble in coming here tonight."

"I'm afraid I caused more trouble than I cured," said the priest. "I seem to have upset both the ghost and Kelly so I don't believe any thanks are necessary; I just wish I could have been of assistance."

Clara Overton, standing alone on her front porch, called good night, almost absently, then went into her house, closing the door and turning off her porch light. Almost immediately the Linden's porch light also went off.

Ben and Bob said a final good night, and their outdoor lights went dark at almost the same moment as Mrs. Terpen ushered the twins through their front door and extinguished the light above it.

The young priest stood alone on the road. He sighed, then crossed himself. "God bless all of those here, all of them. Especially the little one."

As he drove away, the car's headlights parted the

dark like a curtain, then let it close in again, thick and solid. Soda Creek was dark, dark and silent. Until the crying began again.

Chapter 11

Kelly came to breakfast the next morning with eyelids puffy and swollen, hair uncombed and tangled. Her father took one look at her, then put his arms around her. "Kelly? Are you all right?"

"Oh, Dad, she cried all night!"

"I know. I heard her too. And you, Kelly? How long did you cry before you slept?"

"I don't know." Kelly sat down at the table, cradling her head in her arms. "I'm sorry, Dad. I couldn't talk to anyone last night, not even you. I don't know why I feel so upset, or why I'm behaving like a two-year old."

"Not quite," said her father. "Not quite as badly as when you were two. You had tantrums and tears down to a fine art back then." He grinned at her.

An answering grin pulled at Kelly's lips, then faded. "What's wrong with me, Dad? Why do I feel so upset by her, our ghost? Why am I crying all the time lately? I never cry, you know that. What's wrong with me?"

"Here." Alan took a plate of scrambled eggs from the oven, put them in front of her, then sat down across from her. "Come on, eat something."

"I'm sorry, Dad, really. I feel so stupid. That poor priest—and Miss O. must be furious at me."

"It's all right, Kelly. I think they understand, although a phone call or note from you, apologizing, might not be a bad idea."

"I will, Dad. But do *you* understand? Do you know what's happening to me, why I seem to be out of control half the time?"

Alan sighed. "Perhaps I do, Kelly. I'm not a psychologist, but I do read a lot. I think you're identifying with the little ghost."

"Identifying? Oh, you mean I think she's me in a sort of way. But why, Dad? I've never had a thing for ghosts, at least not that I know of."

"You call her 'little one'," said her father quietly. "The name your mother used for you. The ghost is alone, Kelly, alone and lonely. And she doesn't have her mother with her, either."

"Oh, Dad, that's nonsense," said Kelly, but the tears that seemed so ready the last few days threatened to flood her eyes again. She rubbed a hand across her face, trying to force the tears back.

"Maybe it is nonsense, Kelly—and maybe it isn't. I know it took me a long time to come to terms with your mother's death, a long time and a lot of tears. But you haven't cried for her, not since the day of the funeral, never even wept in your sleep. As you just said, you 'never' cry, Kelly and maybe you need to."

"I tried so hard to be strong; I wouldn't let myself cry, Dad. And then I couldn't. But now I want to cry all the time, but I'm not even sure it's because of Mom. The tears just seem to be there, ready, sneaking up on me when I don't want them."

"The little ghost cries a lot, too, Kelly. I think her tears have loosened yours."

"Yes," said Kelly, and let the tears come. "Oh, Dad."

Alan again took his daughter in his arms. "Kelly, Kelly, my poor little one. It's all right, Kelly. Cry all you want to, all you need to. It's all right. I'm here."

After a while, Kelly's tears stopped. Alan reluctantly left for work, already late, unwilling to leave until Kelly insisted he go. And Kelly, realizing that she was too upset to go to school, washed her face, ignored her tangled hair, and went back to bed. In her dreams no one cried —and no one had died.

She woke much later to the sound of knocking on the front door and David's voice, worried, calling her name. "Kelly? Are you there? Kelly? Open the door."

"It's not locked," she called, pulling on her jeans and a sweat shirt. "Come in. I'll be right there."

When she reached the kitchen David was busy scraping her untouched breakfast into the garbage and clearing the table. "Hi," he said. "I met the bus after school this afternoon, but the twins said you'd stayed home. Are you all right?"

"Yes," she said, attacking her hair with a comb. "Or at least I think I am. I slept all day, and feel better now."

"Our little ghost kept you awake all night, too, did she?" asked David. "No one at the commune got much sleep either. I guess the priest frightened her, but she certainly scared my aunt and the other women. I suddenly became the resident expert on our ghost, and had to explain, over and over again, all about her. Or at least as much as I know."

"Sorry," said Kelly, snapping a rubber band around her braided hair. "The priest did upset her. We've never heard her before last night."

"Well, I think you upset Father Glenn," said David. "That was quite a performance you put on. Do you make a habit of grabbing things out of priests' hands? Remind me never to sit near you in church—it could be dangerous."

"I know, I know. I'll phone him and apologize. Don't make jokes about it, David, please. I couldn't handle it; I feel so stupid about the whole thing."

"Okay," said David. "No more priest jokes. But he was only trying to help, you know. We're all trying to help her, I guess, even though we don't know how." He began rinsing the coffee pot, filling it with cold water. "Kelly?" he asked, his back towards her, "Kelly, can we talk? Not about the little ghost, that's nearly all we've talked about since we met. Let's talk about . . . about us."

"Us?" Kelly was surprised. David had come into her life at almost the same time as the little ghost, and had become as much a part of her life as the ghost had. She had never thought about 'us', at least not in the way that David seemed to mean, as if they were a couple. "Sure," she said. "Sure, we can talk. Or at least we can talk until the twins come to check up on us again."

David was adding ground coffee to the pot now, and he still didn't turn around to look at her. "I'm serious, Kelly. Now it's your turn not to make jokes, please." He set the pot of coffee on the stove, turned it on and, his back still to her, said, "I've only known you for three days, Kelly, but . . . but there's been something almost magic about those three days and I . . . I've grown very fond of you. I don't know what to do."

Kelly sat unmoving at the table, a sense almost of fear growing in her, not wanting David to explain, not wanting to hear what he needed to tell her. "I don't understand what you mean," she said in a small voice.

David finally turned to face her, still staying near the stove, the kitchen table between them. His face was serious, his eyes darker than usual, and the smile that could light his face was not there. "I think I'm falling in love with you, Kelly," he said. "And that's ridiculous; three days isn't long enough to get to know a person, to fall in love."

"Oh, but it is, David," said Kelly, the sense of fear lifting. "It is long enough. I know, because I. . ."

"No, don't say it, Kelly, don't say it. Please." His face twisted, almost with pain. "You see, I didn't know this was going to happen to me. I just wanted to be friends, go out once in a while, have someone to talk to and be with. I didn't mean for things to . . . I haven't been fair to you, Kelly."

"Fair?" Again Kelly felt the fear, the uneasiness that she had felt earlier, but she pushed it aside. "Of course you're not fair. All those jokes about my hair and my cooking." She smiled at him, but he didn't smile back.

"No, Kelly. It isn't that. There's . . . well, there's someone else, in Vancouver." The coffee began to perk, louder, faster, as Kelly sat, unable to move, to speak. Louder, faster, then exploding into sizzle and steam as coffee boiled over and hit the hot element.

David turned the stove down. "I'm sorry, Kelly, but I care for you too much not to tell you. I had to let you know."

The spilled coffee had burnt around the edges of the element, and a bitter smell tinged the air in the kitchen. Kelly still sat, silent, her shoulders tense, her hands clenched.

"Kelly? Can't you say something? I'm going home soon and until then I . . . I mean, can't we just be friends? I don't want to give you up, Kelly, don't want to lose you. But it's not fair to you, and it's not fair to Laurie. I have to see her again, explain, settle things in my own mind. Kelly? Please, say something."

The red mist of anger, the same anger that she had felt towards Clara Overton when she told of seeing the little ghost, rose through Kelly again. She clenched her hands harder, fighting against the anger.

"Blonde?" she asked, her voice shaking. "Or perhaps ebony black?"

"What? Oh, Laurie's a blonde, but I don't see. . ."

Kelly stood, her knees shaking, her clenched hands on the table for support. "Thank you for telling me, David," she said formally. "But now I think you should leave."

"Kelly, please. I care for you, very much, but I have a commitment to Laurie, and. . ."

"Out!" Kelly felt her face grow hot as she spoke, and her voice rose shrilly. Her heart was pounding, loudly, too loudly. "Just get out and don't bother coming back. I'm sure you have more important things to do than waste time with me. Go write a letter to your girlfriend or milk a cow or something."

"Kelly, hey. . ." David smiled, his face softening, lit by the smile. "I'm sorry, Kelly, but you should see yourself, your face is as red as your hair. Listen, I'm trying to say that I'm not sure about Laurie anymore, not since meeting you. Can't you understand? Please, don't cut me out of your life just yet. Let me have the rest of my time in Soda Creek with you, let me find out for sure, work through my feelings for you, before I have to go back to Vancouver."

Kelly's heart was beating even louder, so loudly that she was sure David could hear. David reached out a hand towards her. "Please, Kelly?" he said again. "Give me some time? Time—with you?"

Kelly's heartbeats seemed to fill the room, deep and pulsing, an ancient rhythm from the world's past. What was wrong with her, she thought? She was upset, angry, furious, but her heart had never sounded so loud before.

David put a hand to his chest. "Kelly, this hasn't been easy for me. My heart's thumping so loudly that I'm sure you can hear it. Won't you give me a chance, Kelly?"

They stood staring at each other, the kitchen table between them, Kelly flushed, David looking pale and still reaching out one hand towards her, pleading. The beating grew louder and louder, filling the kitchen, bouncing off the walls, reverberating through the late afternoon dusk that filled the room. Then the front door flew open and the twins' voices shrilled through the house.

"Kelly, come quick!"

"It's Indians, a whole bunch of them."

"They've got drums and everything."

"And feathers, and big sticks."

"They're dancing, Kelly."

"They're hitting the drums and dancing, right outside your house."

Chapter 12

Outside, in the growing dusk of the December afternoon, was gathered what looked like the entire Soda Creek Band. Most of them stood silently along the sides of the road, watching, as a group of about ten formed a circle around a pair of large drums, and began to chant. Now the drum beat changed, becoming louder, more complex, and the dancers moved, feet shuffling, bodies following the rhythm, chanting. The onlookers nodded, shuffling their own feet in time to the beat, and the dancers moved more and more energetically, feathered headdresses swaying, belled and tasseled moccasins echoing the drum rhythm, fringed vests and trousers trembling with the movement. The women wore dresses laden with quills, beads and small mirrors; the men, many of them with their hair braided and swaying under their headdresses, wore fringed leggings and short vests that left their arms and shoulders bare.

Kelly and David stood on the front steps with the

twins, watching in amazement. The drummers and dancers seemed unaware of any audience, concentrating fully on their music and dance steps. The chanting rose louder, the spectators from the reserve swaying as they, too, joined in. Kelly caught sight of Ben edging closer to the activity on the road, and saw Mrs. Terpen nervously craning her neck, looking anxious until she caught sight of the twins standing beside Kelly.

"What are they doing, Kelly?"

"Yeah. How come they're dancing on our road?"

"Do you think they're cold? They don't have coats on."

"Do you think they'd let me try the drums?"

Kelly didn't answer the twins, but David did. "I guess maybe they heard our little ghost crying last night too, Tommy. Maybe this is something to do with her. I think they're wearing ceremonial outfits, you know, special clothes to dance in."

"How can dancing help the ghost?"

"Boy, she sure did cry last night."

"I told her over and over it was okay to come and use our bathroom, but she just kept crying."

"David," said Kelly, her anger at him forgotten for the moment, "David, do you think the dancers are trying to do what Father Glenn tried to do last night? Send her away?"

"Wouldn't surprise me, Kelly," he answered. "But listen, she isn't crying. I don't think our ghost is bothered by the dancing, not the way she was by the holy water."

"But they musn't drive her away, not yet!" And Kelly was down the steps, across the lawn and into the middle of the swirling, chanting dancers. "Don't!" she cried. "Please, please don't scare her. She won't hurt anyone. Don't try to chase her away."

The dancers backed away, clearing a space, and Kelly suddenly found herself in the centre of the ring, close to the drums. Every face was turned towards her, dark eyes staring at her solemnly. The drumming slowed, the chanting grew quieter, but the dancers still moved, circling Kelly. "Please," she said again, her throat dry. "Please."

It was almost dark now, and beginning to snow again. Out of the dancers' ranks moved a blurred figure, his long headdress swaying against his knees as he walked, a beaded and feathered spear pointed directly at Kelly. He lifted his other hand and all movement stopped, the dancers standing still, statues freckled with fresh snow.

"We will not frighten the little ghost, Kelly. This is our dance for the dead, to help them go to their spirit home easily. To make them feel that they are not forgotten, even though they are not here. This dance will not hurt the child."

"Basil!" As he spoke, Kelly had recognized the old man. Of course, Joan had said that her grandfather was teaching the traditional native dances to others on the reserve, teaching the dances, the chants, the ways of their ancestors. "I'm sorry. I didn't mean to interrupt the dance. I just. . ."

"It is finished now," said Basil. "We have done what we came here to do. Perhaps tonight the small ghost will not cry. Maybe she will rest."

"Maybe tonight she'll let us get some rest!" One of the onlookers had joined Kelly and Basil, taking Kelly's hand and leading her out of the centre of the circle.

"Joan?"

"Sure, it's me. I don't belong to the dance group, but I like to watch them. Come on, Kelly, you're shaking. Let's get you inside where it's warm."

Then Alan was beside Kelly, his arm around her. "I parked further up the road and walked down," he said. "Couldn't drive through the crowd, and didn't want to disturb the dancers, especially not this unofficial one of mine." He helped her inside where David took her arm and led her, unresisting, into the kitchen.

"Hot coffee," he said. "Sit."

Kelly sat down into a chair, thankful of its support. "Dad?" she asked, but her father wasn't there.

"He's outside, probably talking to Joan and Basil," answered David. "He had some idea of inviting everyone in for coffee."

Outside the house a cheer went up, and Alan burst back into the kitchen. "David, Kelly, get the other coffee pot, the big one, and put it on. See if you can find something for our visitors to eat as well." He was rummaging in a cupboard. "I know we've got a bunch of extra cups in a box in here somewhere. Ah." He placed the sugar bowl from the table, a handful of teaspoons and a carton of milk into the box of cups and carried it all toward the door. "Come on, you two. We're lighting a bonfire by the edge of the road, since there are too many people to fit into anyone's house. Mrs. Terpen's making hot chocolate, and the twins are already handing out cookies. Come on, join the party. Bring that coffee when it's ready, David."

As her father left, Kelly could hear Clara Overton's voice, shrill and piercing. "Alan, what are all these people doing here? I am most DISTRESSED. I drive home from school and find a huge fire practically on my front lawn, and all these people."

"Go and get some of your famous muffins, Clara, and join our guests. The Soda Creek dancers came to help us with our little ghost. Too bad you missed it."

"Well! I do think it is most INCONSIDERATE, but. . ." Her voice faded away.

"Kelly? Come outside with me?" David held the coffee pot in one hand, stretching out his other hand towards her. Kelly walked away from him without answering. She went into the living room and stood, looking out the big picture window. It was too dark to see the Fraser River below her, but she knew it was there, frozen now, still and quiet, waiting for spring. Earlier that day Kelly had looked up at the hills that crouched over Soda Creek. She had once thought of them as a large animal, protecting the houses that nestled against its side. Today, though, they seemed almost to have moved closer to the townsite. She had felt for a moment that the hills were nudging the houses, not protecting them, but pushing them firmly down the steep slope to the river. Somehow she had the sense that the hills, as well as the river, were waiting. Waiting for what? She had shivered, almost afraid.

She heard David sigh, and realized that he, too, had been waiting. "I'm sorry, Kelly," he said, but she didn't answer, didn't turn around, and then the door closed behind him and she was alone.

The bonfire, just off the road and above the bank that led down to the river, was burning well, flames reaching high over the heads of the onlookers, lighting up the faces of everyone who stood near. Kelly caught sight of Bob, his fingers flying over his sketch book. Behind him a small girl, the youngest of the dancers, stood on tiptoe to see, and Bob turned to her, crouching down so she could watch him as he drew. He flipped to a clean page and gestured to the child to step back, smiling, obviously telling her that he wanted her to pose for him. As he drew her picture, others came to watch. The small dancer smiled broadly, and the onlookers nodded their approval of Bob's sketch.

Kelly saw her father, coffee in hand, bent over the open hood of one of the cars that had been parked further up the road, two dark heads beside his, intent on what he was saying. David stood apart from the group clustered around the fire, a slight figure in an oversized jacket, his head bent, oblivious of what was going on around him. The twins knelt beside the fire, two of the children from the reserve beside them, busy with a game that involved sticks, small stones and patterns drawn in the fresh snow. Even Clara Overton had joined the party, and was moving through the crowd, offering a tray of what could only be rhubarb muffins.

"Oh, thank you." The teacher's strident voice carried to where Kelly stood beside the window, watching. "But they're so easy to make, just a few ingredients." Someone offered her a cup of coffee, and she stayed in the centre of a group of women, talking loudly, smiling.

Ben was taking care of the fire, and Kelly saw him through a shower of sparks as he added another log and adjusted the burning pile. Voices rose through the falling snow, voices and laughter, blending into the smell of wood smoke. Someone cheered as Bob finished his sketch of the small dancer and tore it from his pad, handing it to the child with a flourish.

"Me, draw me now. Me," came from the other

children, and the twins stopped their game long enough to see what the excitement was all about. Mrs. Terpen could be heard calling for her children, reminding them that one cup of hot chocolate was all they could have before dinner, but she, too, was engrossed in a conversation with women from the reserve, and her heart didn't seem to be in her nagging. Voices, the snap and blaze of the fire, the quiet hissing of snow falling into flames, laughter. . .

"It doesn't seem right," thought Kelly, still standing unseen at the darkened window. "They're having a party out there, talking, laughing, people who haven't even spoken to each other in years. And it's all because my little ghost cried all night." Would they both, she and the ghost, cry again tonight she wondered?

"No!" she said out loud. "I won't cry. I'll never cry over him, never, never!"

She turned away from the window, tired of the activity outside, tired of it and, somehow, hurt by it as well. She turned her back on the party around the bonfire and there in the doorway to the kitchen, stood the little ghost.

In spite of herself, Kelly gasped, and took a step backwards. "I'm not afraid of her," she told herself, "I'm not!" Taking a deep breath, she went towards the small figure in the red dress, seeing again the ruffled pantaloons, the buttoned high-top boots, the ringlet caught back with a floppy bow.

"It's okay, little one," she said. "I won't let them hurt you. Don't be afraid of me. I promise, I won't let anyone hurt you."

The ghost lifted her arms toward Kelly, just as she had done the first time, holding her arms out as if she wanted to be lifted up. Kelly knelt down and held out her own arms, reaching for the small figure, aching for her, for her loneliness, for her tears. "It's all right," she said again. "I'll help you. Just tell me how, tell me what you want, why you're here."

Slowly the little figure began to grow misty, translucent, the firm edges of her body softening, melting. "Don't go," Kelly called, "Please, don't go."

Slowly, much more slowly than the only other time Kelly had seen her, the ghost faded. But before she vanished completely, Kelly heard her speak. "Emily," she said. "Emily."

Chapter 13

The last trace of the little ghost was still visible, a veil of mist across the floor, when the Linden's front door opened and Kelly heard her father's voice. "Kelly? Where are you?" Alan Linden came into the dark living room, snapping on the light. "All alone and in the dark, Kelly? I had hoped you would join us. Everyone's gone home for dinner now, but I think we all had a good time."

"Not alone, Dad," answered Kelly. "She was here."

"Who was here? That blasted ghost thing?" demanded a gruff voice behind Alan. "That little critter's caused me enough trouble, think she'd know enough to keep away from me."

"Ed Crinchley's home," Kelly's father explained, unnecessarily. "I'm not sure if he's officially discharged, but he pulled up in a taxi a few minutes ago, crutches and all."

The old man came into the house with David, who

had one arm around him and must have helped him up the stairs. "Come into the kitchen, Ed, and I'll see what we can offer you for supper," said Alan, and took the old man down the hall.

David stood in the doorway to the living room, the Linden's empty coffee pot in one hand. "Can I come in too, Kelly?" he asked. He smiled nervously, his dark eyes pleading with her.

And suddenly Kelly didn't care anymore about David's girlfriend in Vancouver. He was here, with her, and she wanted to be with him, talk to him, have him near her. "David!" she said, running to him as if he had been gone for weeks, "David, she was back, the ghost, and she wasn't crying. She spoke, a name, 'Emily', and it took her a long time to fade away."

"Emily," said David. "One of my favourite names. After Kelly." He reached out and touched her cheek. "Hey," he said. "I. . ."

"Kelly, come and give me a hand with supper," Alan called. "And David, if you've got that coffee pot, bring it in and let's get it going again."

As Kelly and David went into the kitchen, her father looked at them questioningly. "Got the problem solved?" he asked.

Ed Crinchley, now settled at the kitchen table, looked up at them. "Problem? Ah, a lovers' quarrel." Then he settled back in his chair is if he were getting ready to watch the argument continue.

"I've seen the ghost again," said Kelly hurriedly, anxious to change the subject. "And she spoke!"

"I'll speak to *her* if she scares me like that again. Cost me a sprained ankle and five gallons of my best crabapple wine."

"But she hasn't said anything before now, Mr. Crinchley," said David.

"No. Just made a blasted racket all last night, so Alan says, so no one got any sleep. Youngsters today don't mind their manners like they used to, ghosts or not!"

"Oh, Mr. Crinchley, please don't growl at her," said Kelly. "She didn't mean to frighten you, and she didn't mean to keep us awake with her crying. I don't think she'll cry tonight; she wasn't when I saw her. Besides, I didn't think you believed in ghosts."

"Growl, eh? So you think the old Grinch growls at kids? Well, I haven't yet, but it might not be a bad idea, especially at those twins." He threw back his head and produced an excellent imitation of an irate grizzly bear.

"How does he know everyone calls him 'the Grinch'?" thought Kelly, then, embarrassed, she went back to the subject of the little ghost. "She said 'Emily'. She said it twice. I wonder if that is her mother's name?"

"I'll bet it's her own name," said David. "Maybe she was just introducing herself to you." He hadn't taken his eyes off Kelly's face since they entered the kitchen, and he was still smiling. Kelly grinned back at him. David might have a girlfriend in Vancouver, but right now he was here, in Soda Creek, with her, obviously thinking about her, caring about her.

"I've been wondering about her, the little one," said Ed Crinchley, his voice unusually quiet with none of its gruffness. "While I was in the hospital I didn't sleep too well. Wouldn't take those fool pills they kept shoving at me, I guess that's why. I kept thinking about her, the way she'd stood there at the foot of my stairs, reaching out her hands. Almost as if she wanted me to give her something or do something for her."

"I think we all feel that way," said Alan from the stove where he was warming up the left-over stew, adding more frozen vegetables to stretch it for the company. "She does seem to want something from us. I wonder why she doesn't just come right out and tell us what it is?"

"Maybe she isn't an experienced enough ghost yet," said David thoughtfully. "I mean, tonight was the first time she spoke, last night was the first time she made any sound at all. Maybe she's learning how to be a ghost, and will tell us when she can."

"Or maybe she's just too little, hasn't learned the words for what she wants," said Kelly. "She's only about two years old, remember."

"What can a thing that size want around here?" said Ed Crinchley.

"Well, she sure didn't want any holy water," commented David.

Kelly blushed. "Come on. Let's forget it."

Seeing Ed Crinchley's puzzled look, Alan explained how Clara Overton had brought a priest out the night before, and how the ghost's crying had begun as he was about to sprinkle the holy water. "They heard her everywhere, even down at the reserve, which is why they came to do their dance for the spirits. She liked that better than the holy water, I guess."

Her father hadn't mentioned Kelly's contribution to both events, but David did. "You should have seen Kelly, Mr. Crinchley. She tore that water right out of Father Glenn's hand, and then she barged into the middle of the dance, yelling at them to stop. She really stood up for her little ghost."

Kelly wasn't angry at him. "The Lindens have always been fighters, David," she said softly. "One way or another, we usually get what we want, and we aren't afraid to fight for it."

Alan looked surprised at his daughter's words and the smile left David's face as he answered. "I get the feeling you do, Kelly," he said. "You're a strong person."

Ed Crinchley had not been paying attention to the conversation, and now he interrupted. "What does she want here? Do you have any idea, Kelly?"

Kelly shook her head, and the old man returned to his usual gruff manner of speaking. "Well, I ain't going to have her crying all night again, the way you say she did last night. Won't have it."

And the ghost didn't cry that night, or the next or the next. But she did visit everyone who lived in the town, in the commune and on the reserve. Over the next four days the community became quite accustomed to her standing quietly in their bedrooms, kitchens, garages, on their snow-covered lawns, in their gardens, beside the school bus stop. Standing, reaching out and, once in a while, saying, "Emily, Emily." She no longer frightened people; no one jumped back, startled, as Ed Crinchley had done, no one was hurt because of her. She seemed to stay longer when she appeared, and it took her much more time to fade away when she left.

Even Clara Overton, with a front lawn liberally sprinkled with holy water, had several visits from the ghost. "I do believe the child is STARVING," she told Kelly. "She watched me make a batch of muffins, and she stayed until they were out of the oven. I'm sure she wanted one, poor thing."

The ghost came to Ben's garden, standing beside the carefully pruned and staked raspberry bushes, peering through the leafless branches. She visited Bob in the small workroom in his house, and watched him as he formed a large bowl on his potters' wheel.

At the commune, she most often appeared in the barn, seeming to like the cows, and she was always on the Soda Creek Reserve when the dancers held their practices.

Alan found her beside his car in the early morning as he scraped his windshield clear of ice, and Kelly saw her at least twice a day; in her bedroom, beside her chair as she watched T.V., waiting for her in the hall as she came home from school or beside her bed last thing at night.

Ed Crinchley must not have growled at her after all, for the small apparition went often to his home. His sprained ankle kept him confined inside, unless someone helped him down the stairs and along the icy road of the townsite. Kelly suspected that the Grinch was becoming rather fond of the small ghost, even though he complained loudly about the nuisance she was.

"Poor little critter," the old man said one night when Kelly took him some dinner. "She just stares at you. Almost begging you to do something for her, whatever it is. And it's the strangest thing. Seems to me that I've seen her somewhere before—must be she reminds me of someone—but I can't think who."

For four days the community seemed to be waiting, waiting for something to happen. No one made any more attempts to get rid of the ghost, yet no one was completely at ease with her around. They accepted her presence, weren't frightened when she appeared, talked about her, wondered about her. Yet everyone knew that she couldn't stay, that sooner or later they had to find a way to make her leave.

After all, they couldn't live with the little ghost forever. Or could they?

Chapter 14

Again it was Saturday night, almost a week since Kelly had first seen the ghost. "Such a short time," she thought, "such a very short time to have made my life so different."

She thought about how she had spent this Saturday night—a movie in Williams Lake with David, driving his uncle's car. He looked unfamiliar in slacks and a sweater rather than the jeans and oversized jacket he wore around Soda Creek. After the show, Cokes and hamburgers and the long drive home, David, holding her hand, turned to smile at her once in a while, the lights of oncoming traffic brushing over his face.

"You look better," Kelly had said.

"Yes. I feel better, too. Much stronger. Haven't had to spend an afternoon just resting since . . . since I met you." He had squeezed her hand and smiled. "You must be good medicine, Kelly."

David hadn't tried to kiss her as he saw Kelly to her

front door, just stood and looked at her, finally reaching out and, a finger under her chin, tilting her face to the light. "Kelly. . ." he said, then shook his head, mumbled good night, and left.

Kelly's father had been waiting up for her, feet on the coffee table, T.V. on. "Hi," he said. "Have a good time?"

"Yes," she had said, "a great time." They had watched T.V. together for a while, then Alan had gone to bed. Kelly, however, wasn't sleepy, and she sat in her room, working on a watercolour, a larger picture of the little ghost.

It grew late, but Kelly found herself reluctant to go to bed. Then she realized that, subconsciously, she was waiting for the little ghost to appear. It had been just a week since she had first seen the ghost, and over the last few days almost everyone in and around Soda Creek had seen her. She was no longer Kelly's personal apparition, but Kelly was waiting for her, wanting to see her, somehow knowing that she would come to-night.

Kelly stood, pushed the picture to one side, and stretched. She thought for a moment, then went quietly into the kitchen, and as she took the first step over the threshold, she saw the small figure standing beside the fridge.

"I knew you'd be here tonight," Kelly said happily. She knelt down, bringing her face to the same level as the child's, and smiled. "Hi, Emily. I'm glad you've come to see me again. What do you want, little one? Can you tell me?"

Again, the ghost reached out her arms towards Kelly, the golden ringlet falling against her cheek as she did, the red velvet bow swaying slightly. "Emily," she said. "Emily home. Please? Emily home?"

Kelly held out her own arms, reaching, yet afraid to move any closer. "Please?" said the ghost again, and she took two small steps towards Kelly, her high button boots sounding loud on the kitchen floor. She was close enough to touch.

Kelly shifted her weight and leaned forward, her hand brushing the little ghost's cheek. There was a sense of coldness, ice, sliding up Kelly's arm, numbing her fingers. Then the ghost smiled and lifted her own small hand, placing it firmly over Kelly's. "Please, Kelly," she said. Then she left; fading, becoming misty, before vanishing completely.

For a long moment Kelly knelt there, her arm stretched out. Then she sighed and stood up. Her hand was icy cold, and she went to the sink and ran warm water over it. "She came to me," she thought. "She came to me, she let me touch her. She knows my name. She is my ghost, no matter how many others have seen her."

* * * * *

Once again the sun through her bedroom window woke Kelly on a Sunday morning, the sun and the sound of voices in the kitchen. "But Alan, we can't just let the matter rest. We can NOT go on being known as the community with a ghost. I know she's a dear child, but. . ."

It was Clara Overton. Kelly smiled to herself. This was how last Sunday had begun. She dressed, quickly braided her hair, and went into the kitchen. "Morning,

Dad," she said. "Morning, Miss O. Isn't it a great day?"

"You're in a good mood this morning," said her father.

"Oh, Alan, girls her age are always in a good mood when. . ." The rest of the teacher's comment was drowned out by a loud banging at the front door.

"Hey," shouted a voice, over the noise, "Hey! Give me a hand. Can't get up these steps by myself."

Kelly and her father both went to open the door and were nearly hit by a crutch. Ed Crinchley leaned against the narrow side of the porch, one of his crutches stretched out in front of him, aimed at the door. "Morning," he called, tucking the crutch back under his arm and hobbling around to the stairs. "Got myself down my own stairs okay, but don't seem to be too good at getting up these ones."

Kelly and her father helped the old man into the house, wondering what he would do when he saw Clara Overton. But to their surprise, he just nodded at the teacher. "Morning, Clara. The muffins were fine."

"Oh, thank you, Ed." Kelly watched in amazement as the teacher hung her head and blushed. "I'll make you some more today, or maybe you'd like to join me for dinner? I've got a lovely roast with potatoes and. . ."

"Sure." The Grinch settled himself in a kitchen chair and beamed up at Clara Overton. "Haven't had a meal like that in years."

"Um . . . well, it's nice to see you two getting on," said Alan as he brought another mug and poured coffee.

"I decided it was time to let bygones be bygones, ever since Clara brought me that first plate of muffins," said Ed.

Again there was a knock at the door. "Hello," called Ben, letting himself in. "Hope we're not intruding."

"I found that pattern I was telling you about, Clara," said Bob, so excited he ignored Kelly and her father and went directly to the teacher. "Look at this!" The two of them began to spread bits of paper, yarn and canvas across the kitchen table.

"Hey, Ben," said Ed Crinchley. "I finished that book you lent me. You got some more interesting reading material at home? Those mysteries ain't bad to read."

Kelly went into the living room, returning with two extra chairs. "What is going on here?" she wondered. "A week ago these people wouldn't even speak to each other, and now they're behaving like long-lost friends. What is happening?"

She got back to the kitchen in time to hear Clara Overton inviting Ben and Bob to share the roast she was cooking for dinner. "There's plenty for everyone," she said, then, remembering Kelly and her father, she turned to them. "And for you two as well. Oh, do come. It's been so long since I've cooked a meal for company."

"Why, she's hardly said a word in capital letters this morning," Kelly thought. "And she's not wearing that thick make-up today."

Alan was declining the invitation. "I'd like to take Kelly into town for dinner, Clara. It's sort of a tradition —at least since last Sunday. But will you have some breakfast with us?"

"All we need is David to make the pancakes," Kelly said and, as if on cue, the doorbell rang.

"Hi. Can we come in?" David led the way, followed by his uncle George and a small, slender woman.

"Oh," said George, surprised. "Sorry. I didn't realize

you had so many visitors already."

"That's no problem, George. We were just wondering if David would show up in time to make the pancakes." Alan tossed the package of mix across the room. "Catch, David. Looks as if we're feeding a crowd this morning."

David stood awkwardly, holding the package of pancake mix in his hands. "Uh, sorry, we thought. . ." He stepped back to stand beside the slender woman. "This is Naomi," he explained. "She's a friend, from the island, Vancouver Island. She came to. . ." He seemed uneasy, unsure of what to say.

Naomi moved forward. She had grey-streaked hair that stood out around her face in a halo of frizz, looking as wiry and uncontrollable as Kelly's own hair. She wore a large pink sweater and baggy grey sweat pants with worn spots on both knees, and her cheeks were as pink as her sweater. Setting a large, embroidered handbag on the floor, she held out her hand to Kelly. "You must be Kelly," she said. "Yes, David was right about you. You do radiate strength; strength and emotion. I'm pleased to meet you, pleased to meet all of you," she said, one hand clasping Kelly's, the other gesturing broadly to include the rest of the group.

Kelly stared at her, amazed. "Radiate?" she asked. Naomi turned back to her and smiled, and Kelly saw with a shock that one of her eyes was a deep sky-blue, and the other was the dusty green of September grass.

"Of course, my dear. But then she really is your ghost, isn't she? She came to you first, so David says."

"David? George?" Alan looked confused. "Who is. . ."

"Oh, I'm sorry, Alan," said George. "I thought David

had explained. Naomi has come to help us with our little ghost. She's had a lot of experience with this sort of thing."

"Indeed!" sniffed Clara Overton, the capitals back in her voice. "And just what KIND of experience has she had?"

"Oh, my. Oh, dear." The small woman looked at David and George sternly, and they both stared at the floor. "You two haven't been fair, you know. Not fair at all. Now, explain me to your friends, and let's get on with things."

"Uncle George, you. . ." began David, but his uncle retreated to the far corner of the kitchen, leaning against a counter, shaking his head.

"No way, David. She's your mother's friend. You explain."

"And do hurry up, David. I would dearly like a cup of coffee before we begin." Naomi shook her head and sat down on the nearest unoccupied chair.

Everyone turned to look at David. "Well," he said, "you see, I thought Naomi would know what to do. . ."

"Oh, David. You haven't warned these people at all, have you?" Naomi shook her head again, frowning. "I'm sorry that I was sprung on you like this," she said. "I thought you knew. I've come to help with your ghost. I'm a witch."

Chapter 15

The kitchen was completely silent after Naomi's announcement, awkwardly and uneasily silent. David looked at Kelly, apologetically, Bob and Ben exchanged amused glances, Alan Linden still seemed confused and Clara Overton's mouth had dropped open, frozen in a wide, silent 'OH'. Only Ed Crinchley didn't appear affected by the presence of a self-proclaimed 'witch' among them.

"Sure," he said, breaking the silence. "One of those Wicca followers, I bet. There's a real nest of them on Vancouver Island, I hear."

"Naomi's a white witch, a good witch," David said. "She's been a friend of my mother's for years. Actually, she's my godmother, sort of."

"David Stanton, you, of all people, should know better! There's no such thing as a 'white' or a 'black' witch. It is how the power is used, the energy directed, the outcome—a fire that warms a cold house we think of as 'good', while a fire that destroys that same house we label 'bad'. The energy, power, the 'fire' is not in itself either. . ." Naomi stopped, rubbing a hand through her hair. "Sorry," she said. "I seem to go into that lecture automatically, and I know David's heard it far too often."

She smiled at Ed Crinchley. "You used the term 'wicca'. Yes, I am a follower of the Goddess and the 'wise craft', and it is her power I use, letting it work through me to help others."

"Mr. Crinchley," asked Kelly. "How on earth did you know about 'wicca' being witchcraft?" Kelly had barely been listening to Naomi, her attention focused on the old man whose rough ways and language had always led her to believe that he was uneducated.

Everyone had turned to look at Ed Crinchley, and every gaze was as curious as Kelly's. She had not been the only one to notice the incongruity of the Grinch's comment.

"Hey!" he said. "Mind your own business, all of you."

Naomi, too, was staring at the old man, and she nodded her head and smiled gently. "You have a hidden life," she said. "I see a bear who is forced out of his dark cave into the light, and growls and snarls at having to leave his safe hiding place."

Kelly gasped aloud, thinking of the uncannily accurate imitation of an irate grizzly bear that the Grinch had produced in that very kitchen only a few days ago.

The old man glared at the witch-woman as if he were going to growl at her, too, but Alan stepped in, trying to bring the conversation back to safer ground. "Naomi, this is Ed Crinchley. He's lived in Soda Creek for many years. And. . ." he continued, "you seem to know Kelly, but perhaps the rest of us should introduce ourselves. I'm Alan Linden, Kelly's father." He stepped forward and offered his hand, self-consciously formal. "I'm pleased to meet you, Naomi."

The slender woman took his offered hand, but instead of shaking it, she turned it upwards, cupping her white fingers around his work- roughened ones, turning his hand so the palm faced her. "You are a strong man, Alan. But it is time you laid your guilt to rest. It was never your burden to bear."

Alan went pale and took a step backwards. Father and daughter looked at each other, eyes wide. The accident that had taken Kelly's mother's life had been caused by a tire blow-out on an icy freeway. Although he had only spoken of it to Kelly once, and never to anyone else, Alan blamed himself for his wife's death, for not keeping her car in better repair.

"No one knows that he feels responsible for that accident," thought Kelly. "No one but me knows that." How did she, this small woman with the pink cheeks and strange eyes, how did *she* know of this secret guilt?

Ben and Bob, sensing that something unsettling was happening, took their turn at being sociable. "I'm Ben. . ."

"And I'm Bob. Hi." They stepped forward, and Naomi took one of their hands in each of hers, again refusing to give a formal handshake, but holding their hands, turning them upwards and cupping them in hers.

"A strong blood kinship," she said, smiling. "Not so very different, except on the surface. Both of you work with the earth, I sense, but somehow in different ways."

"That's right," said Ben, the surprise showing in his voice. "I'm an avid gardener, and my brother works with clay, which is 'earth' as well. George must have told you about us."

Still leaning against the kitchen counter, George shook his head. "No," he began. "I haven't. . ." But no one was paying any attention to him.

This time it was Clara Overton's turn to gasp aloud. "Your BROTHER?" she said. "You two are brothers?"

"Of course," said Bob. "I thought you knew. Our last names are different, as I go by my mother's maiden name professionally—with the pottery and the studio and everything. I thought it sounded more 'artistic' than our father's last name."

"But we thought . . . we never . . . I mean. . ." Miss Overton fell silent, speechless.

Again, Alan stepped in. "No, I don't think any of us realized that you and Ben were related."

Naomi turned her strange eyes towards Clara Overton. "And you?" she asked. "Will you not come and shake my hand and bid me welcome?"

"No!" said the teacher, loudly and unexpectedly.

"Naomi, this is Clara Overton," said Kelly's father. "She teaches at the high school in Williams Lake and she. . ."

"Don't tell her anymore about me, Alan, don't, please!" To Kelly's astonishment the teacher seemed near tears, and she cowered back in her chair, almost as if she were afraid of the stranger.

"Clara, I am pleased to meet you. Blessed be. I sense your trouble, but now is not the time nor place to speak of it. Perhaps, later, you will take my hand and we can talk, alone. I think I can help you put your memories to rest."

"How can you, how can you know?" Clara Overton began to cry softly, quite unlike her tears of a week ago. Last Sunday she had cried noisily, dramatically, clutching Alan's arm and dabbing at her thick make-up with a handkerchief which she waved wildly to add emphasis to her words. Today she sat almost silently, tears flooding her eyes but her mouth only moving slightly, emitting tiny moans, with no make-up streaking on her cheeks as the tears fell.

"I am sorry," said Naomi. "I don't mean to cause pain for anyone. Perhaps it would be better if I left now."

"No," said Miss Overton, brushing her hand across her eyes. "Please don't go because of me. I'm so sorry. I don't know what came over me. Please, Naomi, stay and help us with our little ghost. And . . . and perhaps I could talk to you later, maybe tomorrow? Just the two of us?"

"When you are ready, I shall be there," answered the small woman.

"Miss O. has a secret too," thought Kelly. A secret such as her own father's guilt over her mother's accident and the secret that the Grinch was hiding in that 'cave' of his. Somehow Naomi had sensed something about Clara Overton, something that the teacher seemed afraid she would reveal in front of the others.

"The coffee's ready," said Alan. "I think we could all use some, and maybe some breakfast, too." There were murmurs of "thanks, but I've eaten, just coffee, please," and Kelly's father began burrowing in a cupboard, looking for extra mugs.

The atmosphere in the kitchen changed as Alan began to serve coffee, everyone talking, everything seeming normal once more.

"Naomi arrived late last night," David explained to Kelly. "She saw the ghost, just for a minute, when she was getting out of her car. Naomi really *is* a witch, you know."

"Well, she seems to know things that no one else does," said Kelly. "Do you think she can help our ghost?"

"Could we all go outside, do you think?" Naomi stood, her coffee mug in her hand. "I would like to see some of the places your little ghost appears. And there are others who know her too, aren't there? I see another of her friends, a strange person, a child, yet a child who has a strong second personality, a split, division or. . ." Again she rubbed a hand through her hair. It crackled with static electricity, standing out even further from her face. And the twins arrived.

"Boy, are there ever a lot of people here."

"Can I try your crutches Mr. Grin . . . Mr. Crinchley?"

"Are you making pancakes again, David?"

"Ah. I understand. Twins." Naomi smiled at the children. "Hello. We are going to see the places where the little ghost likes to visit. Would you come with us, since you are her friends too?"

"Sure. She likes it by the school bus stop."

"I can show you our bathroom, it's tidy today."

Outside the sun shone and the air was warm, almost balmy, with no hint of snow. They all gathered on the plowed road in front of Kelly's house, coffee cups in hand except for Ed Crinchley whose mug was carried by Tommy, still hoping for a chance to experiment with the crutches. Almost automatically everyone grouped themselves in a circle around Naomi, and stood waiting, silent again.

She took a deep breath, her mug cradled in her hands, the steam rising gently around her face, catching in her hair. "Someone's coming," she said, nodding down the empty road in the direction of the reserve. "Someone who also cares for the little ghost." As the words left her mouth, a car that no one else had heard, turned the corner and stopped near the group. Basil and Joan got out.

"Grandpa said there was something going on down here," said Joan. "I think he just wanted another cup of coffee."

"Basil's right," said Alan. "Basil, Joan, this is Naomi. She's come to help us with our ghost. She's a. . ."

"I'm a witch," said Naomi cheerfully. "Blessed be."

"You're not a witch!" said Tommy vehemently.

"Witches are ugly, and they never wear pink stuff."

"And it isn't Halloween."

The twins had missed Naomi's introduction, and they stared at her in disbelief. But Basil raised his right arm in salute, and spoke rapidly in Shuswap.

"He says welcome," translated Joan. "He welcomes you in the name of our people, and says that he feels the spirit of the old ones working through you."

"I thank you, Basil," answered Naomi. "I feel the strength of you, a great strength."

Basil nodded at her, solemn. "It is good that you have come. The little one, she grows stronger every day. Soon she will be too strong in this world to be able to return to the spirit world."

"Yes," said Naomi, "I know."

"But she says she *wants* to go home!" Kelly spoke up, remembering that she had not yet told anyone about the ghost's most recent visit to her. "She came last night, to the kitchen, just like the first time I saw her, and she said, 'Emily home'."

"She spoke to you again, Kelly?" asked Bob.

"Yes. She said 'home' and. . ."

"What else, Kelly, what else did she tell you?" Naomi like everyone else, was watching Kelly.

"She said 'please home'," answered Kelly, not meeting the woman's mismatched eyes. "And she said my name . . . and she let me touch her."

"Ah. That is why you carry her presence with you so strongly." Naomi nodded, as if she suddenly understood something that had been puzzling her.

"Please, Naomi, do something for her. She wants to go home so badly."

The witch looked intently at Kelly. "Yet I feel that you don't *want* her to go home, Kelly. Do you really wish her to leave?"

"Yes!" Kelly's was not the only voice answering the question.

"It's not that we don't like her," explained Miss Overton, her voice so low that she could scarcely be heard. "But she needs her mother."

Once again the teacher had said something completely out of character, and once again Kelly was astonished. "How can Miss O. know that?" she wondered.

"I think you are right, Clara. You have insights where small children are concerned, insights and love," said Naomi. "But now, show me where your ghost likes to visit, and tell me about her."

The group with the unlikely-looking witch made its way slowly up and down the main road of Soda Creek, stopping at Ben and Bob's house, standing in the garden, looking through the winter-withered raspberry canes as Ben explained where the ghost most often appeared to him. They visited Bob's studio, admiring the bowl the little ghost had watched him forming, staring at the potter's wheel as if it might suddenly begin to rotate on its own.

Ed Crinchley made the others stay outside his house, but he allowed Naomi to enter and peer down the red stairs to the grimy basement as he relived his first visit from the ghost. Mrs. Terpen was taken aback when the twins, followed by a crowd of people, arrived at her door, asking to see the hallway near the bathroom. She somewhat nervously allowed the twins to show Naomi around, obviously puzzled by their comments that this lady wasn't at all like the witches on T.V.

Clara Overton encouraged everyone to tour her immaculate home, and handed out muffins as the group listened to her tale of the ghost-child who had watched her so carefully as she baked.

Outside the teacher's house, Naomi was still for a long time, then walked and stood on the snow-covered lawn, on the exact spot where Father Glenn's bucket of holy water had landed. "She was hurt here," the woman said, "but it was a hurt in her spirit life, not one from her life on earth. She isn't upset about this anymore."

David whispered to Kelly, who was avoiding his eyes. "I didn't say a word about flying buckets. But I'll bet Naomi could tell us how all that consecrated water ended up on Miss O.'s front lawn."

"David Stanton, keep your mouth shut," hissed Kelly, and Naomi's mismatched eyes swung towards her, almost as if she had heard.

The witch-woman listened to the stories of the

ghost's appearances, nodded, and once in a while asked a question. She would stop sometimes and close her eyes, tilt her head to one side much like a grey robin, seeming to be listening to something only she could hear. For almost an hour the group led her around, almost believing that this small woman with the unruly hair *could* do something about the little ghost.

The sun slipped behind a cloud, the temperature dropped. "Let's go in," Naomi said. "I don't think there is much more for me to learn out here." She strode towards Kelly's home, but near the jailhouse she stopped, turned off the road, and went towards the old building. She bent her head under the low doorway, and stepped carefully across the threshold.

"Be careful," called Alan hurrying after her. "I started to do some work on the floor. A few of those boards are ripped up, and some of them are just too old and rotten to take any weight."

"Stay there, please. I shall take care." The wiry grey head disappeared into the gloom inside the decrepit building.

Outside, everyone waited for what seemed like a long time. Alan kept peering anxiously into the doorway, concerned for the witch's safety, but he didn't enter the building. At last Naomi reappeared, blinking in the daylight, her hair even wilder than it had been. She looked pale, the pink spots on her cheeks now a much lighter shade than her sweater, and she reached gratefully for Alan's offered arm.

"No one's seen the ghost in there," said Tommy.

"No. She doesn't like it there." Trisha's voice, like Tommy's, was unusually quiet.

Naomi agreed with the twins. "You're right. She

doesn't like it in the jailhouse. There is no trace of her presence in that building. Yet there is pain, great pain, and grief and confusion. Almost insanity. And it is connected very strongly to her, your little ghost. I must go now and rest. Please forgive me."

"But what are you going to do, what should we do, Naomi?" asked David.

"David, for now I must rest. Perhaps I shall understand more later." She shook her head, as if shaking away an unhappy thought, and began to walk towards the commune. George hurried after her, taking her arm, and the two of them moved slowly away.

But then Naomi stopped, and turning back, called, "Mr. Crinchley, you have the answer you know. Only you don't realize that you have that knowledge. It is buried somewhere deep in your private cave, and in order to find it you will have to invite others into that world of yours. But you, and only you, can help the little ghost."

"Mr. Crinchley? What is she talking about?" Kelly's voice rose sharply, angrily. "What do you know, and why won't you tell us?"

All eyes turned to the old man, balanced precariously on the snow-covered edge of the road, his crutches propping him erect.

"Blast the woman!" he shouted. "She should mind her own business. Blast her anyway!"

Chapter 16

Ed Crinchley pushed through the group of people, his face tight, his crutches slamming into the road.

"Mr. Crinchley, we don't want to interfere, but Naomi says you know the answer—or can find it. What does she mean?" Kelly followed the old man towards his home. "Please, Mr. Crinchley. You heard what Basil said. Soon Emily won't be able to get back to the spirit world at all."

"A man likes his privacy. That woman's got no right telling you things about me."

"But, Ed. . ." Alan stood beside his daughter, outside the Grinch's home. "Naomi didn't tell us anything about you. She just said you had some knowledge. . ."

"And 'a little knowledge is a dangerous thing.' Especially for those who ain't got no business knowing it."

"That's a quote, Mr. Crinchley, from Pope, the poet. I didn't know you knew any poetry." Kelly was astonished.

"Look, ain't nothing wrong with getting educated. Nothing wrong with not bragging about it to people, neither." The old man had reached the foot of his own front stairs, and turned, glaring at Kelly and her father.

"You two going to help me up these blasted things, or you want me to crawl up?"

Alan took one of the crutches, and slipped his arm under the old man's shoulder. "We'll help you, Ed. You know we will. I wish you would help us, though."

Without answering, Ed Crinchley pushed open his door, grabbed his crutch away from Alan, and hobbled inside, slamming the door behind him. The twins had followed, keeping a safe distance behind, but now they ran to Kelly and her father.

"Boy, is he grouchy."

"He's really being a Grinch today."

"What's the matter with him, Mr. Linden?"

"Yeah. He was snarly at the witch-lady."

Alan sighed. "I don't know what his problem is, kids. Oh, well, there's nothing we can do about it, I guess."

"But Dad, it's peculiar. He knew what the word 'wicca' meant, and he quoted Pope just now. That's not at all like Mr. Crinchley." Kelly was as puzzled as the twins.

Joan and Basil stood by their car, ready to leave, Ben and Bob beside them. Clara Overton was quiet, standing alone, deep in thought, and David sat on the fence outside Kelly's house. Everyone looked up as Kelly and her father returned, the twins in tow.

"I don't know what Naomi thinks Ed knows about our little ghost," said Alan, "but he certainly is upset about her saying anything about him."

David jumped down from the fence and came to Kelly. "Hey," he said. "Let's forget about it for now. How about a walk while it's not too cold. Come on, Kelly, no point in getting upset over the Grinch."

A door slammed and a loud shout echoed down the road. "All right, blast it. Get over here and let's start looking for that fool bit of information I don't know I have." Ed Crinchley stood on his front porch, calling to the group. "Come on," he said. "I guess the old bear can open his cave to you, at least until we figure out what to do with the little critter."

"Raincheck on that walk, Kelly," said David. "Let's go find out what's in the Grinch's cave."

"Come on in," said the old man, stepping back from the doorway as everyone arrived. "The place is a bit of a mess, but I'm not much on cleaning up."

The house had a musty smell, overlaid with the peculiar, unpleasant odour of wine fermenting, and could have used a good cleaning. "In here, not the living room, here, in my study." Ed Crinchley threw open a door part way down the narrow hallway, and went in. "I guess what that woman thinks I know has to be here somewhere in my research files," he said.

"Files? Research?" Kelly felt a bit like *Alice in Wonderland,* with things getting 'curiouser and curiouser' all the time. Why would the Grinch bother with files?

The room was large, probably the original living room of the old farmhouse, and was lined on two sides by full bookcases. Against another wall stood a bank of four filing cabinets, and a corner held a stack of cardboard boxes, overflowing with yellowing papers. In the centre of the room was a table with an old typewriter, and beside it, neatly stacked, a thick pile of typed pages.

"Every blasted fool thinks he can be a writer," grumbled the old man. "Got me my degree in history years ago, and been writing this fool book ever since."

"You write books?"

"Like Stephen King?"

"Do they make movies of your books?"

"Do they have pictures in them?"

The twins seemed relatively unaffected by the Grinch's announcement, but the adults stared at him in amazement. "You went to university?" asked Clara Overton.

"You're writing a book?" said Bob, and Ben repeated the question.

"Mr. Crinchley, why on earth haven't you told us? It's almost as if you were ashamed of going to university, of having an education." Kelly spoke for everyone.

"Taught in a big school once, back east. Didn't like it. Came home here, after my father died, and thought I'd write a book about him; about the early days of Soda Creek and how his father came here in the eighteen-sixties. Then I kept on finding more and more stuff, people would give me things, old newspapers, books, family journals, pictures—and now I got too much information to put in one little book. These blasted filing cabinets, they eat things I put in them, and I never can find the right document when I need it."

"An historian," said Joan. "You're Soda Creek's historian!"

"That explains why you know so much about the early days around here, Ed," smiled Alan. "But Kelly is right, you know. It's nothing to be ashamed of."

"Don't want anyone to call me an intellectual. Bunch of wimps and snivelers. I like my life here, and I just sort of play at this research and history. Keep thinking that one day I might get that book finished. Then I don't know what I'll do with my time."

"That's what Naomi meant by you having a secret life, being in a 'cave'," said David. "And somewhere in all this information must be that 'knowledge' that will help us find out about the little ghost."

"Guess so." The old man looked around him vaguely. "It's all Cariboo history, not just Soda Creek but the whole area, all those books and files. Maybe there is something in there, but I haven't got a notion as to what it is, or where it would be."

"Well," said Alan thoughtfully, "what if we each take a book or some files and read everything in it? Maybe we'll know what we're looking for when we find it."

"Go ahead, help yourselves, if you think it will do any good," agreed the old man.

Within a few minutes everyone had found a spot to work, and had selected something to read. Clara Overton organized things, setting up a system of recording what had been gone through, reassuring Ed Crinchley that everything would be put back exactly where it had been found. She located a box of old photographs for the twins to burrow through as their contribution to the search, then, once everyone had settled down to read, she left the house, returning later with a large platter of sandwiches.

Ben sat at the table, intrigued with files on agriculture, exclaiming to himself once in a while as he discovered something unusual; a plant he hadn't suspected would grow in Soda Creek, the number of carrots produced to feed the busy town in its prime, the weight of the largest squash grown in the area seventy-five years ago. It seemed that then, as now, Soda Creek's microclimate had produced some excellent crops.

Alan had chosen a thick pile of documents containing old bills and invoices for machinery parts and repairs, and descriptions of mining techniques in the early days. He, too, quickly became absorbed in what he was reading.

Bob chose a large armchair as his work area, the arms of the chair piled with books on weaving, quilting patterns and other crafts used by early settlers of the area.

Another drawer of a filing cabinet held writings about the first inhabitants of Soda Creek, the Shuswap Indians, and Joan read furiously, taking notes once in a while, her mind probably as much on current land claims as on the traditions and lifestyle of her ancestors. Basil had smiled and confessed that his eyes weren't too good, so he sat crosslegged on the floor beside the twins, keeping a semblance of order to their rummagings through the photographs.

David and Kelly shared a box of unidentified material, finding catalogues, letters, receipts, wedding invitations and diaries. In one of the diaries Kelly lost herself, becoming caught up by the life of another girl in Soda Creek, but many years ago.

Mrs. Terpen arrived at the door around three in the afternoon, looking for the twins, worried, as they hadn't shown up for lunch, an event almost unheard of. Reassured that the children had eaten, she left, taking a couple of thick folders with her and promising to go through everything in them. After she had gone, Kelly put down the diary she had been reading, and stood up, stretching. The others looked up, their faces expectant.

"I'm just stretching," explained Kelly. "I haven't found anything—or at least I don't think I have. How can we know if we've found it if we don't know what we're looking for?"

"I understand exactly what you mean," said her father. "This is fascinating to read, but I don't know what good it will do. What on earth did Naomi think we'd find in this collection of Ed's?"

"It's rather overpowering, all this information," said Clara Overton. "These old recipes I found are wonderful, but there is so much information here."

"It will take us days to go through it all," agreed Joan, "and then we might miss it anyway, because we don't know what it is."

The twins had been conscientious in their search through the box of photographs, but they, too, were becoming discouraged, and more than slightly bored. "It's just a stupid old bunch of pictures," said Tommy, pushing away the pile in front of him.

"Yeah. I thought it would be more exciting."

"Does the witch-lady really think there's a clue in all this old stuff?"

"Yeah. A real clue, like in mystery shows on T.V."

"This is dumb. I'm going home." Tommy stood up, and Trisha followed his lead, handing the pictures in her hand to Basil. But as she stood, a photograph which she had not noticed slipped from her lap. She bent to pick it up, saying as she did, "Boy, they sure wore funny clothes in those days."

"Come on," said her brother. "Let's go ride the skidoo before supper." But Trisha didn't answer, just stared at the picture in her hand.

"What is it, Trisha?" asked Kelly, taking the old photograph from the child. "What is it?"

A man, a woman and a child, stiffly posed, looking awkward in what were probably their best clothes, stared up at Kelly from the picture. The woman sat on a chair with an elaborately carved back, the man held a top hat in the crook of his left arm, his right arm lying possessively on the woman's shoulders. And standing between them with one hand on the woman's lap, was a small girl in high-button boots, lacy pantaloons that peeked out from under her dress, and long ringlets, held back with a bow.

Trisha's words echoed Kelly's thought. "It's her. It's the little ghost girl!"

Chapter 17

Everyone crowded around Kelly who held the photograph in her hand. "Trisha's right," said Alan. "It is our little ghost."

"I think that's the very outfit she wears when she visits us," added Clara Overton. "A shame it's not a colour photograph.'

"Let me see." Ed Crinchley was trying to struggle to his feet from the armchair. Kelly took him the picture, and he stared at it dubiously. "I guess it's her, all right," he said. "But blast if I know where this picture came from. And who's that with her? Her parents, I guess. I wonder what their names are."

"Sara and Jonathan," said Tommy, and as the adults stared at him in amazement he explained sulkily. "It says their names right on the back. No one's let *me* see the picture yet."

Ed Crinchley turned the picture around, held it for Tommy to see, and squinted at the writing on the back of it. Behind him, Kelly, too, looked down at the words.

"Emily," said Kelly. "It *is* her name. It says, 'Sara, Jonathan and Emily Hyde.'"

"Hyde. Hyde . . . something's stuck in my mind about that name, but I can't seem to unstick it." Ed Crinchley was shaking his head, his brow creased in concentration. "Jonathan Hyde. Now what was it. . ." He squinted at the writing on the picture, his eyes narrowing as he thought.

Clara Overton spoke softly. "Sara Hyde must have been an unusual woman." Everyone looked at her, surprised. "I mean," said the teacher, "I mean, not many mothers would dress a child that age in a red dress. Maybe pink or blue or. . ." She stopped talking, and stared down at the picture again. Kelly noticed that Miss O.'s cheeks were flushed.

"You're right, Clara," said Bob. "It *is* a strong colour for a child, most unusual."

"A strong mother, a strong child—and a strong, fighting spirit," added Basil. "Yes, I begin to see why the ghost-child is so powerful."

Everyone was quiet for a moment, intent on the photograph, until the twins became restless.

"Is that all?" asked Tommy.

"Isn't there more writing on it?"

"Is that the clue?"

"And I found it, Tommy, all by myself! I found the clue."

"It's a stupid clue," answered Tommy. "I think it's dumb. I'm going home."

"Tommy's mad because he didn't find it," giggled Trisha. "I'm going to go tell Mom how *I* found it." The door slammed behind them as the twins left.

Alan took the photograph from Ed Crinchley's hand, staring for a moment at the brownish portraits on the front, before turning it over and studying the back. "The names are faded," he said, "and they were written in ink. See, there's an ink spatter near Emily's name. But there is something else written here, down near the bottom. Numbers? Yes, letters and numbers. 'JH:4:27', at least I think that's what it says. It's been written with a ballpoint pen, so it has to be modern."

"Here. Give me that thing." Ed Crinchley again reached for the picture. "That's my writing," he said quietly. "I must have written it."

"Well, what does it mean?" asked Ben. "There's got to be a reason why you wrote it."

"Yes," repeated Bob, "what *does* it mean, Ed?"

"That's easy," said Joan. "It's obvious. JH—those are the initials for the father's name, Jonathan Hyde."

"Sure, that's it," said David. "It's his initials."

But Ed Crinchley sat silent, his head bowed. "No," he said quietly, "no, I'm sure that's not right." He rubbed a hand across his forehead, and Kelly saw that he was pale, and that there was a beading of sweat on his face. Alan noticed it, too. He put a hand on the old man's shoulder.

"Ed," he said, "Ed, are you all right? What's the matter?"

"Blast it, anyhow. This getting old sneaks up on a person." Ed Crinchley handed the picture to Kelly and reached for his crutches. "Those numbers, letters—it's some sort of a system I used to have, to do with filing and cross-referencing things. Haven't used that system in years. How do you expect me to remember something like that?"

"He's forgotten!" thought Kelly. "He's forgotten what his code means."

"You look tired, Ed," said Alan, helping the older man to his feet. "It's no wonder you can't remember anything right now, with all this confusion around you and your ankle probably hurting as well. Why don't we all take whatever we're reading home, and do our research there, leave you alone to get some rest."

The old man looked drawn, deep pain lines around his mouth. He nodded gratefully at Alan, and hobbled out of the room, not saying a word.

"Oh, poor man," gasped Clara Overton. "He's forgotten. He knows it's important, but he's forgotten!"

"Don't worry about it," said David, trying to be cheerful. "He'll probably remember after a good night's sleep. It's a technique I use all the time when I'm studying. Leave it to the subconscious."

"Perhaps he will remember, David," said Ben. He and Bob, their arms full of file folders and books, were getting ready to leave.

"Perhaps," echoed Bob. "But don't forget he *is* an old man, and people forget more as they get older."

Basil spoke from where he still sat, cross-legged on the floor beside the box of photographs. "Yes, we forget. But sometimes we remember what others have forgotten."

"And," said Joan, "we know our ghost's last name, so we can keep on reading. But now we can watch for anything to do with the name 'Hyde', instead of just reading aimlessly."

The others nodded in agreement, and began to assemble their own selection of historical material to go through that night. Kelly replaced the diary she had been reading, putting it back in the box where she had found it. "I can't do anymore tonight," she said. "It's school tomorrow, and I've got algebra coming out of my ears. I *have* to do some homework."

From the kitchen came the sound of running water. "I hope Ed's taking one of those 'fool' pills," said Alan. "A sprain can hurt more than a break, and he hasn't let himself get much rest."

"I'll go and make sure he's all right," said Clara. "I think a nice hot cup of tea might be just what he needs." The teacher hurried down the hallway towards the kitchen, and the others called goodbye as they went out the front door.

"Want to join us for dinner in town, David?" asked Alan as they walked up the road. "We've found a restaurant in Williams Lake that makes superb cheesecake."

"Sounds great. Just let me check in with Uncle George. I'll be back soon—around five okay?"

As David headed off towards the commune, Kelly turned to her father and again tried to smile. "Thanks, Dad, but you didn't have to invite David, you know."

"I know, little one, but he's a nice, cheerful young man, and you look as if you could use some cheering up. I figured dinner with David and me would be twice as beneficial. We'll coax a smile out of you yet, see if we don't."

"Sorry to be so miserable, Dad, but I feel as if we came close today, close to finding out what little Emily wants and why she is here. First Naomi, knowing so much without anyone telling her, then the Grinch and all his records and information. Then. . ."

She stopped, staring off into the distance, down the

road. "Then what, Kelly?" asked her father.

"Then the Grinch—Mr. Crinchley—couldn't remember why he had written those letters and numbers on the back of the picture. You could see he was upset, hurting, angry at himself for not being able to remember. He *has* to remember, Naomi said he had the knowledge that would help, but he can't remember, and no one can help him. We are so close, yet no closer than we were yesterday to finding out about our little ghost."

"Don't forget what David said." Alan put an arm around his daughter's shoulder in a comforting hug. "Maybe Ed will remember what that code means, once he's had a good sleep and feels better."

"Maybe. And maybe he won't, and he'll just hurt more because he can't remember, and the rest of us will have to keep on reading through his files, hoping we'll stumble across whatever it is we need to find."

"It will work out, Kelly, I know it will. Come on, get yourself beautiful for your date with the two most eligible men in Soda Creek this evening. Let's not talk about it anymore, let's just worry about whether or not Barvarian chocolate cheesecake is on the menu again tonight."

"I'll try not to think about it, Dad. I'll try. But I don't make any promises, chocolate cheesecake or not."

Kelly had tried, pushing all thoughts of the tiny ghost out of her head as they drove to town and ate dinner. And, in spite of herself, she began to feel happier, more content. As David and her father talked and joked, she found herself laughing with them, enjoying the meal, enjoying their company, enjoying her second Sunday dinner out with no dishes to wash. All three of them arrived back in Soda Creek full, happier, and with the stress of the day's happenings forgotten for the moment.

"Thanks for the dinner, Mr. Linden," said David as he got out of the car. "Is it all right if Kelly walks me part of the way home?"

"Afraid of ghosts, David?" smiled Alan, then added "Sure. Enjoy your walk. But don't be long. Kelly still has her ears full of algebra, and tomorrow is a school day." He went into the house, turning on the front porch light as he closed the door behind him.

"Good to see you smiling again," said David as he tucked his arm through Kelly's and they started down the road towards the commune. "You got quite down this afternoon."

"Dinner fixed me right up," laughed Kelly. "Do you suppose chocolate cheesecake is addictive?"

"Probably only for redheads," answered David. He stopped walking and the two of them stood under the large fir tree that shaded Ben's front lawn. "Redheads are addictive themselves," he said, seriously. "I find them very addictive, especially Soda Creek redheads."

"I thought you preferred blondes," snapped Kelly, remembering David's girlfriend in Vancouver.

"Not anymore, thank you ma'am. I've developed a sudden and. . ." He took her face in his hands, tilting it towards him. "A sudden and deep, very deep, affection for a Soda Creek redhead." He bent to kiss her, his eyes dark in the night, his hands gentle and warm against her cheeks. And from the night shadows of Ben's garden, someone giggled.

"Those twins! I've had it with them!" David's hands dropped from Kelly's face, and he strode towards Ben's tidy picket fence, peering into the garden. "Tommy!

Trisha! Get out of here, you two. Go home."

Again came the giggle, louder, this time from somewhere above Kelly's head. "Are they in that tree?" asked David, moving back to the tree, craning his neck to see into the meshed branches. "I don't know how you put up with those two, Kelly. They need a good spanking."

He looked up angry enough to climb the tree and administer that spanking himself. Kelly put a restraining hand on his arm and said, "It's not the twins, David. Listen."

Again came the soft laughter, louder and longer this time, the high, sweet laugh of a very young child. "It's not the twins, it's her," Kelly said.

David listened, still looking up into the branches above him. "So it is," he said. "I'm glad she's happy tonight. Maybe she's pleased that we've found her picture, maybe she knows that we're trying to help her. But enough is enough!"

He put both hands on his hips, and called out into the branches, his voice stern. "Emily Hyde! Shame on you."

"Emily," said Kelly gently, "go and visit someone else for a while, please. Goodnight, Emily."

"Goodnight, Emily," David repeated firmly.

The laughter faded, and the ghost was gone. David turned to Kelly again. "Now where were we?" he asked.

Chapter 18

David was waiting for Kelly at the school bus stop the next afternoon. Somehow, she had known he would be. "You're late," he said, taking her school bag from her, reaching for her hand.

"It was the twins," she explained. "They got into a fight after school with some other kids, about ghosts being real or not. They were still in the principal's office when the bus got there to pick them up."

"It's all your fault, Tommy. I'm going to tell Mom."

"Not my fault. *You* told them we had a picture of our ghost." The twins rushed past, ignoring Kelly and David.

"Sounds as if those two are in trouble," said David. "I hope Mrs. Terpen lets them come to the meeting."

"Meeting? What meeting?"

"The one Naomi wants to have tonight. It's been a busy day around here, Kelly."

"What's happened?" Although most of Kelly's

thoughts during the day had been for David, suddenly all of her concern for the little ghost flooded back. "She hasn't gone, has she? Emily? Not without saying good-bye to me, she wouldn't do that."

David squeezed her hand. "No, she's still here. And she seems happy. She's been popping up all over the place saying, 'Emily home,' to everyone, giggling the way she did last night. I guess she knows something the rest of us don't."

"David, what's happened?" Kelly sat down on the split rail fence around her yard, zipping her coat against the cold.

"The Grinch remembered something," said David, propping one foot up on the lower rail of the fence beside Kelly. "He phoned Uncle George this morning, so excited he could hardly talk, and hollered for 'that Naomi woman' to get over to his place right away."

"Did he remember what his code on the back of the photograph meant?" asked Kelly.

"He won't say," answered David, "at least, he hasn't told anyone except Naomi. She was over at Miss Overton's when Mr. Crinchley called Uncle George and. . ."

"That's right. Miss O. wasn't at school today. Is she sick?"

"I don't think so," said David. "I suspect she just wanted a chance to talk to Naomi alone. Remember, she asked her if she could. Miss O. phoned our place even earlier than the Grinch did, and Naomi went off to see her right after breakfast. Then, just after the Grinch phoned, Mrs. Terpen got on the party line talking to someone in town, so I had to walk over to give Naomi the Grinch's message. That's how come I was there and got to see what was going on. Miss Overton had been crying."

"Do you think she's all right, David?"

"I think so. She wasn't crying when Naomi left, and she gave her a big hug and thanked her. Then she did something really peculiar. She took off that big charm bracelet she always wears, and put it down on the table, and said, "See, Naomi. I shall put my memories away."

"I wonder what she meant, and what she told Naomi," Kelly wondered out loud, remembering the teacher's fear of what Naomi could sense of her private life. "I guess we'll never know. Anyway, go on. Then what happened?"

"I haven't a clue," said David. "I walked with Naomi to the Grinch's house, and went home. How am I supposed to know what they talked about?"

"David! You're not being fair. What about the meeting?" Kelly stood shivering. "It's too cold out here. Come on in and tell me the rest."

As David washed and Kelly dried and put away the Lindens' morning dishes, David told her the rest of what he knew. About noon, Naomi had come back to the commune, smiling. But all she had said to anyone was, "It will be all right now. I know what has to be done."

"That's all she said?" asked Kelly.

"Yes. Except the next thing I know, I'm over at that old community hall with Uncle George and Miss Overton, knocking down cobwebs, sweeping the floor and setting up chairs. Miss O. got the kitchen cleaned up, and Uncle George started a fire in that big wood heater in there."

"The community hall? I don't understand." Kelly was puzzled. The community hall hadn't been used for years, although it had once served as the centre of Soda

Creek's social activities, hosting bingo games, potluck suppers, parties and dances. But that had been before the people in the community had gone to war, given up speaking to each other, long before she and her father had moved away from Ontario. Kelly had never been in the old building, never seen it open, the whole time she had lived in Soda Creek.

"We need the hall for the meeting," explained David. "Naomi says that she knows what has to be done, but that everyone has to help. She wants us all, everyone who has seen the little ghost, to get together while she explains what she and Mr. Crinchley discovered, and then she'll tell us what we have to do. The community hall was the only place big enough to hold everyone, which is why I spent the day cleaning it."

"When is the meeting, David?" asked Kelly, now eager to find out what had been learned about little Emily.

"Seven o'clock. You and your Dad are in charge of coffee, so you'd better bring those extra cups of yours."

"But is that all you know, David? You mean you've been here all day while I've been at school, with unfinished algebra homework, thanks to you, and that's *all* you've been able to find out?"

"That's it," he admitted. "That's everything I know. Naomi says she'll tell us all together this evening, and the Grinch isn't talking to anyone. That's every single thing I've been able to find out, except. . ." He looked at Kelly and his face changed, the lightness draining from it. "Except I have to go home too, Kelly. Back to Vancouver. Tomorrow. She phoned and she wants me home for Christmas. We haven't had time to think about it but Christmas is only five days away and. . ."

But Kelly had stopped listening. "She! She has to take you back, take you away, just when . . . Oh, I hate her, I hate her!"

"Hate her? My mother? Kelly, what's wrong with you? Mom phoned because it is near Christmas and she wants me home, with my family."

"Your *mother?* Oh." Kelly turned away from David, staring down into the dishwater, trying to hide the blush she could feel spreading across her cheeks. "Sorry," she said, her voice nearly inaudible. "I thought. . ."

"You thought it was Laurie who wants me home. Oh, Kelly. You're still jealous, in spite of everything, in spite of last night. Here." He turned her towards him, his hands on her shoulders. "I told you, Kelly, I told you last night. You're addictive, and I'm hooked. There's no one else anymore, not Laurie, not anyone." He kissed her gently. "No one but you, Kelly," he said again.

"Sorry," said Kelly, "sorry, I. . ." And then the full impact of what he had said struck her. "You have to leave," she said in a small voice. "You have to leave. Tomorrow."

"Yes," he answered. "But I'll be back, Kelly. I promise."

"When?" Kelly's voice shook as she asked the question. "When will you be back, David?"

"After Christmas, for a bit. I've got to get back to university, Kelly. With being sick, I've lost some of my year, but I can pick up a few courses that start in January."

"And after that? After the term is over? Will you come back this summer?"

"Yes!" His voice was sure, and he pulled her close to

him. "I'll come back as soon as my last exam is over. I'll find a job around here; maybe at Gibraltar Mine . . . maybe Uncle George can hire me as official cow milker or something. I promise I'll come back, Kelly."

Again he bent to kiss her, but she twisted her face away. "I wonder, David. I wonder if. . ."

The front door slammed behind the twins. "Kelly, did you hear?"

"The Grinch remembered all about the photo."

"Yeah. He and the witch-lady are making a meeting for everyone tonight."

"We're going, and Mom and Dad too."

"Mom says we're going to find out how to make the ghost go home."

"It's going to be like a good-bye party for the Emily ghost."

Kelly pushed away from David. "Both of you," she said. "You and Emily, you're both leaving." She turned her back, walking away from him, not hearing him call her name, walked down the hall towards her bedroom saying over and over again, "Both of them, both of them."

"Wait, Kelly, listen. . ." David followed her, pleading, but his words made no sense. She pushed open the door of her room and there, perched on her bed smiling, was the little ghost.

Kelly took two slow steps towards the tiny figure. "Emily," she said, "Emily, don't go. I don't want you to leave. Stay here. Please, don't leave, not you too."

"Kelly!" David had come into the room behind her and he put an arm around her waist, pulling her to him firmly. "Kelly, don't do that to her. She *has* to go, you know that. Both Basil and Naomi think that the stronger she gets here, in this life, the longer she stays here, the harder it will be for her to go where she belongs, where she wants to be. Don't try to keep her here, don't let her see you cry because she's leaving."

Kelly turned to look at him. "I can't let her go, David," she said.

"You can, Kelly. You can, and you must. I know how hard it is for you. But you love her, don't you? Show your love. Let her go."

"Kelly?" said the small ghost, the smile fading from her face, her eyes widening into tears. She reached out her arms to Kelly, the way she had that first night, the bow around the golden ringlet swaying as her body moved. "Emily home? Please, Kelly?"

David was right, Kelly knew that. And Clara Overton had been right, too, when she had said that you can't keep a ghost around as if it were a stray kitten, no matter how much you wanted to. And why, Kelly wondered, did she want so badly for the little ghost to stay in Soda Creek? Why did the thought of Emily leaving upset her so much?

It didn't matter. A 'party' was what Trisha had called the meeting tonight. A good-bye party. No matter how much it hurt, Kelly knew that she had to smile, to encourage the little ghost to leave Soda Creek, move out of the real world and go back to whatever insubstantial, spiritual or ghostly place she belonged. A good-bye party. Not a funeral. Not like when her mother. . .

"I know, David," said Kelly softly. "I know I have to. I'll try." She stepped closer to the ghost, making her lips say words that her heart didn't wish to be said. "Yes, Emily. You're going home. We're all going to help you go home."

The small ghost's face changed again, the smile that she had worn so frequently in the last few days returning. Then she wavered, grew translucent, and was gone.

"I know you'll miss her, Kelly," said David, his arm tightening around her.

A small hand tugged at Kelly's arm. Beside her, Trisha turned her white face upwards, her own eyes as tear-filled and wide as the ghost's had been a few minutes earlier.

"I don't want her to go away either," whispered Trisha. "I want her to stay here with us always."

Kelly put her arm around the girl and hugged her. "I know, Trisha. We're all going to miss her." "And I'll miss David, too," she said to herself. "Both of them, I'll miss them both so much, so very, very much."

Chapter 19

The temperature dropped steadily through the late afternoon, and by seven o'clock when people began to gather at the community hall, the heat from the wood furnace that George had stoked earlier in the day was welcome.

Kelly and her father were among the first to arrive, Alan Linden worried by Kelly's pale face and strained, tense voice. But he asked her no questions, just stayed near her, watchful.

"It's all right, Dad, really it is." Kelly had become aware of her father's concern as they filled the large old coffee urn that belonged to the community hall. "Don't worry about me. I'm being unreasonable, getting upset about Emily leaving. Maybe I am doing whatever you called it—identifying—with her. But I do feel miserable, even though I'm not being logical."

"I wish I could help, Kelly." Her father spoke gently. "Try to remember that this *is* just a ghost that we're talking about. We've all gone from not believing in ghosts to feeling as if this ghost were a part of our family. It doesn't make any sense at all."

"I know, Dad. The whole thing is crazy. But . . . but, David has to leave tomorrow, too."

"I'm sorry, Kelly. I hadn't realized. . ." began her father, but Clara Overton bustled into the kitchen, unaware that she had interrupted.

"Oh good, I'm glad you figured out how to work that percolator; we're going to need a lot of coffee tonight, it's so cold. I've made rhubarb bread instead of muffins, thought it would go further. Help me slice it, would you Kelly, and see if you can find some big plates. We've got several batches of cookies coming as well, and Joan said she'd bring something, but I'm not sure exactly what." She busied herself slicing thin pieces of rhubarb loaf, hands moving surely, quickly, quietly. As David had told Kelly, Clara Overton no longer wore the charm bracelet that used to jangle with the teacher's every movement.

Ben came in carrying two large jugs, filled with a pink liquid. "Hi, everyone. I thawed some raspberries and made a punch for anyone who doesn't want coffee."

"I've brought my largest pottery bowl for it," said Bob, depositing a huge blue and white bowl on the counter. "But we didn't have any cups. I hope someone's got some."

"Right here," said Alan. "I brought every cup in our house."

As Kelly buttered slices of rhubarb bread, she could hear voices in the main hall as more and more people arrived. The twins' excited chatter rose over the buzz of adult conversation, and she heard Ed Crinchley's gruff voice saying, "Don't you kids badger me, now. You'll find out about your ghost same time as everyone else does, not before."

Joan came into the kitchen, handing Kelly a large tray covered with plastic wrap. "Smoked salmon," she said. "Hope you like it." She disappeared back into the hall.

"Oh, there's Father Glenn," said Clara Overton. She handed the bread knife to Kelly and rushed off to welcome the young priest. "I'm so glad you could come tonight, Father. It seems as if we are going to solve our problem after all."

"I hope so, Clara." The priest's voice was troubled. "I've been most concerned since my visit here, most concerned for everyone. I hope everything will work out."

Trisha stuck her head into the kitchen, calling loudly. "The witch-lady's here. Come on, Kelly, Mr. Linden. Everyone's sitting down, and the Grinch and the witch-lady are getting ready to tell us."

Kelly followed her father out of the kitchen, and they slipped into the last row of chairs that David and George had set up that afternoon. The community hall was crowded, the chairs almost all taken. Among a group from the reserve, Kelly recognized some of the dancers. The smallest dancer sat beside Bob, turned towards him, and Bob, sketchbook in hand, seemed to be once again drawing her picture.

Some of the faces were unfamiliar to Kelly, including several whom she assumed came from the commune. She saw George, and guessed that the dark haired woman beside him was his wife, David's aunt.

Basil sat stiffly upright on a chair in the front row, his hat resting on his knees. The twins, placed firmly between their parents, sat unnaturally still, leaning forward, straining with anticipation.

Naomi moved calmly to the front of the hall. "Welcome, everyone," she said. "Blessed be." She looked around her, nodding, as if she approved of what she saw. "I am glad all of you have taken the trouble to come here tonight," she said. "It will need the help of all of you, everyone who has seen and loved the little ghost-child, if we are to be able to send her home." She rubbed a slender hand across her forehead, as if she were tired, or in pain.

"Ed has asked me to tell you what he discovered about your ghost, a story he partly remembered, then dug through his files to substantiate. Without him and what he has been able to find out about Emily Hyde, I suspect it would not ever be possible for her to leave."

She paused. "I know. Many of you may be thinking that perhaps you don't want her to go away, that she has become part of your lives and you want her, need her here with you. But remember that she has been asking to go 'home'; it is something she wants. We must respect her wishes, no matter how much it hurts us personally."

She looked directly at Kelly as she spoke, and Kelly found herself lowering her eyes, unwilling to meet Naomi's mismatched gaze. David slipped into the empty seat beside Kelly and reached for her hand. "Cows got loose again," he said. "Have I missed anything?"

"No, we've just started," answered Kelly, as Naomi continued.

"Let's begin with Ed's story", she said, "because it

really was the beginning of everything. I shall tell it to you, not the way Ed uncovered it, through an old newspaper clipping buried in his file on the Soda Creek jailhouse, but as it must have happened. That way, perhaps, it will seem more vivid to you, and you will understand better why the little ghost is here, and what she wants of you."

"Jailhouse!" said Tommy. "The clue on the back of the picture. 'JH' and then those numbers. It means *jailhouse!*" He sat back in his seat proudly, unaware of his mother's attempts to keep him quiet.

"You are right, Tommy. Ed says the 'JH' did mean the jailhouse, and the numbers were references for his files on it. Once he remembered that, he was able to find the rest of the information we needed.

"In the beginning, it wasn't an unusual story; just the story of a young family, Jonathan and Sara Hyde and their small daughter Emily. Ed couldn't find out where they came from, or why they were in the Cariboo, but he did discover that they were strangers to Soda Creek, just travellers passing through. The only dates we have are a few days in October, 1879. A few days mentioned in the old jailhouse records that Ed found in a box of material given to him by someone a long time ago."

"Can't remember who gave it to me. Doesn't matter. Not important to remember that," growled the old man.

"No, you did remember what *was* important, Ed, that's what counts." Naomi smiled gently before continuing her story. "We know that the Hydes spent one night in Soda Creek after arriving on a stagecoach that had brought them up the Cariboo Road. From Soda Creek they planned on continuing their journey on one of the sternwheelers that made their headquarters here. Those boats, as you know, took passengers and freight up the Fraser River, a river too treacherous to be travelled safely until it reached Soda Creek.

"The gold rush in the Cariboo was nearly over by then, so it is unlikely that Jonathan Hyde was taking his family to Barkerville in the hopes of finding gold. Perhaps he had a job offer in Quesnel or Fort George—we don't even know his trade. Maybe the Hydes came to visit relatives, or perhaps, just to travel, although Ed doesn't think that too likely, given the state of the roads in those days. We'll never know just why the young family was in Soda Creek, or where they were going when they boarded the boat that October morning. But, according to a newspaper report of the incident that was with the jailhouse files, the river was unusually high and turbulent that fall, and, as the steamer pulled away from its mooring, the child, Emily, fell from the high deck and was swept away by the strong current."

"She drowned? Oh, no!" Kelly had spoken aloud without realizing it, but no one turned to stare at her. Both David and her father put an arm around her, and she heard others in the group gasp as they learned how their little ghost had died.

"Yes, Kelly." Naomi's face was solemn. "The strength of the current made it impossible to rescue her, and onlookers reported that she vanished from sight within seconds. She died in the river; alone, cold and frightened.

"The newspaper said that her body had not been found, at least not at the time the article was written, four days later. The writer of the article expressed doubts that her body would ever be found. I believe he was correct."

Naomi was silent for a moment, almost as if she were gathering her strength for what she must now tell. Then, she continued, "Sara Hyde screamed when her daughter fell from the boat and, before anyone could stop her, she leaped from the deck into the river in an attempt to save her child. The newspaper says that she cried 'Emily, Emily, Emily' three times before she, too, was swept away—and drowned."

"Oh, no!" This time it was Clara Overton who voiced the feelings of the group. Father Glenn, sitting beside her, crossed himself before reaching out to lay a comforting hand on her arm. Trisha had begun to cry softly, and from where she sat, Kelly could see that Tommy's head was bent, his shoulders moving, as if he, too, fought with tears.

"I know, Clara. It is painful for me to tell you this, as it is for you to hear. All of us feel for the small child and her mother. Now I have to finish the story, and I am afraid the unhappiness is not yet over."

"The father. Jonathan." Alan Linden was sitting forward in his chair, his face white, his thick eyebrows seeming darker against his paleness.

"Yes. Jonathan. A man who has lost not only his wife, but his child as well, and in such a manner, has a great deal of grief to bear." Naomi's eyes were on Alan as she continued. "Perhaps Jonathan felt guilt for some reason, perhaps he only suffered and mourned. He left the boat, which had put back to shore after the accidents, and made arrangements for his wife's burial, for her body was recovered almost immediately. Then he disappeared, and no one in Soda Creek saw him for a few days.

"His story begins and ends three days later, in the

jailhouse, where, 'mad with grief' as the newspaper reported, he was taken after having been found walking the streets of the town late at night, weeping, crying, calling for his wife and child. Perhaps the authorities were afraid that he would lose control of himself, turn against other people, harm them or their property. Perhaps he had already done something that made him a public menace, some irrational act stemming from his grief. He knew no one in the town, and had no one to take him in, to offer him comfort and shelter. He was locked safely away in the jailhouse and, the next morning when the jailer returned, Jonathan Hyde was found hanging from a beam in his cell."

"Ah. My heart aches for him." This time it was Basil who spoke aloud.

There was silence in the hall, then Ben asked quietly, "But Naomi, knowing how Emily and her family died, knowing this, what can we do? I mean. . ." He shook his head, puzzled.

"Sara Hyde and her husband were buried; someone bid them a final good-bye, said their names aloud and wished them peace. But Emily has not been recognized in that way, in a ceremony such as a funeral. Her body was never found. And, shortly after her death, there was no one left in this world to mourn for her, to remember her. I feel sure that that is what Emily wants; to be remembered, to be grieved for, and to be reassured that she was and is loved on this earth. I think she wants to be told good-bye."

"Not a funeral, no!" Kelly's voice was loud, and she stood as she spoke. "No, I can't, I can't. . ."

"No, Kelly. You have had your share of funerals, and little Emily would not ask you to go through that again. She needs our good-byes, our assurance that it is all right to leave us, to go where she wants to go. Not a sad occasion, a positive, reassuring ceremony, both for her and for us."

"It's not happy to say good-bye." Tommy sounded belligerent, and Trisha echoed his feelings.

"What's so great about saying good-bye?"

"It will be hard, Tommy, Trisha, but I know it is what Emily wants. I will tell you what I think we should do, what will release the small ghost, and then I shall leave to let you discuss it among yourselves and reach a decision as you share food and drink. In many ways I am an outsider here, and the decision about what you want to do for Emily must be made by you, by the community.

"Tomorrow is the 21st of December, a date that, in almost all religions, marks the start of a time of celebration. In the Wicca tradition, one of the names of this time is 'Yule', a word used by Father Glenn in his own church's celebrations. Tomorrow, the 21st, is the winter solstice, the longest night and shortest day of the year, and the human race has always celebrated this day as a renewal of the spirit.

"Tomorrow night will be a powerful time to say good-bye to Emily. I think that once she understands that she is loved and that she will be remembered, then she will leave, gladly. I will share with you the pattern for a ceremony we can use, and ask each of you to make your own good-byes to her, using that pattern. Listen."

Naomi began to speak softly, chanting words that blended together into poetry that was almost music. "Think of the pattern, the flow, of what I just said.

Think of the rhythm, the sound, the chime of the words, and think of the things that *you* want to say to Emily. I know you will find it easy to write your own good-byes to her, should you choose to do so."

She turned, and walked past the rows of chairs, her hair bristling around her face, seeming to move on its own with some sort of electrical force. At the door of the hall she turned back. "Places absorb emotions from the people who use them," she said. "As I felt Jonathan Hyde's agony and insane grief in the old jailhouse, so I now feel happiness and joy from this building; as if it has stood empty for too long, and now rejoices that you all are here. Whatever pain you feel at losing your small ghost, remember that she has brought you together. You have found each other, you know. Blessed be."

The door swung behind Naomi as she left the hall, caught by a gust of wind, and Kelly went to close it. As she stepped outside, reaching for the solid wooden door that had banged back against the wall of the building, she watched Naomi's slight figure walking down the road. The sky was clear but Naomi's hair seemed a wiry cloud caught in the moonlight. Kelly took a step down the stairs of the community hall, hesitated, then called, "Naomi."

"Yes, Kelly." The witch-woman turned, waiting, and Kelly had the feeling that she knew what her question was even before the words were spoken.

"Naomi, why now? Little Emily's been dead for so long. Why did she choose *now* to come back?"

"Perhaps someone mourned, not for her but for another one who is gone. Perhaps there is another good-bye that has not yet been said, Kelly, another death that someone here in Soda Creek has not come to terms with, has not accepted. Perhaps Emily came so that through her, *that* good-bye could finally be spoken and the grief of the one who mourns so deeply could at last be eased."

Kelly didn't speak, but inside something seemed to swell and grow, pushing against her heart, her throat.

"There is much power in tomorrow night, Kelly. Perhaps, with Emily's help, you can say your good-byes, both to Emily and to the one for whom you still grieve so deeply, so strongly. The Goddess be with you, child. Blessed be."

Naomi, looking almost as translucent as the little ghost, the moonlight seeming to shine through her, turned the corner of the road and was gone.

Kelly stood by the still open door, aware of the smell of hot coffee from inside the hall, and the sounds of voices as food was passed and shared.

"Another good-bye," Naomi had said. And tomorrow, the 21st of December, would be the third anniversary of Kelly's mother's death.

Chapter 20

The next day Clara Overton brought candles, thick white candles that she clustered on a table at the front of the community hall. "My classes made them," she explained. "We've sold some of them for Christmas gifts, but I thought . . . I thought she'd like them here, tonight."

David, George and others from the commune had spent the morning in the woods, cutting dense, heavy, evergreen branches which they looped, wreath-like, against the walls and spread among the candles on the table. The hall smelled of the outdoors; pine, fir and cedar mingling their scents together.

Earlier in the day a group from the reserve had scrubbed and waxed the wooden floor of the old hall, until it caught and reflected the gleam of the overhead lights, the smell of fresh wax blending with the evergreen scents.

The twins, allowed to stay home from school to help

with the preparations, had discovered a roll of white satin ribbon in their mother's sewing supplies, and had spent a great deal of time painstakingly tying small white bows to the evergreen branches hung against the walls.

Kelly, too, had not gone to school. She had wandered over to the hall several times, listlessly straightening an awkwardly tied satin bow or holding a ladder steady while branches were put into place, but she hadn't stayed long on any of her visits. She and David had gone for a walk after dinner, both of them quiet, their infrequent words spoken in low, almost hushed voices.

"Kelly," he said. "It's all right, Kelly. I will come back, I promise. Everything will be all right."

"Will it, David?" Kelly had asked, and he had nodded his head, but not spoken his answer. He kissed her again outside her front door, holding her hand, looking at her as if he was trying to memorize her face.

"I'll see you at the ceremony," he said as he left. Both of them knew that David was to leave that night, that they wouldn't be alone together again. Both of them knew, but neither of them said good-bye.

By eight o'clock it was completely dark, the full moon hidden behind thick clouds that promised to bring snow before the night ended. Silently, people began to gather in the community hall, summoned by the sounds of dancers and drums. One small light showed from the kitchen; otherwise, the only illumination in the hall came from the banked candles on the table, now lit and guttering silently every time the door opened.

Basil and his people, in full dance regalia, moved slowly, solemnly, in a circle around two drums, their steps measured, their chanting muted. Even the tiniest, lightest dancer seemed to move heavily, and as the hall filled, people grouped around the dancers, silent, watching.

Kelly stood near the door, her father on one side of her, David on the other. "Tomorrow we'll bring in a tree," said Alan. "Clara thinks it would be a good idea to have a Christmas Eve party, with small gifts for everyone, sort of a community Christmas. Basil has offered to teach us the friendship dance then, so we can all join the dancers, share with them."

"Yes," said Kelly. "But tonight is a different kind of sharing, isn't it, Dad?"

"Ah, little one. I know how hard this day is for you. I . . . I find it difficult too."

"I know, Dad."

A gust of wind set the candles flickering again as the door opened and Naomi came in. She stood near Kelly, watching the dancers, and Kelly wondered how the dim lights in the room could pick up the colours of her eyes, one blue, one green, so clearly.

"Kelly, are you ready?" The strange eyes swung towards her.

"Yes," said Kelly after a moment. "I think so, Naomi."

Basil had seen Naomi enter, and he gestured to the drummers who fell silent. The dancers stopped, moving to the edge of the hall. The drummers picked up their skin-covered drums, placing them against a wall, leaving the centre of the room empty.

Naomi nodded at Kelly. "Let us begin, then," she said, and stepped into the centre of the hall.

"We are here to say good-bye to Emily Hyde," she

began. "I ask you all to come closer to me, to form a circle, to reach out and take each other's hands."

Silently, the group moved inwards, towards the slender woman. Kelly held her father's roughened hand, David's hand firmly clasping hers on the other side. She caught a gleam of white against a dark suit, and watched Father Glenn, beside David, reach out to take Clara Overton's hand. Ed Crinchley stood without crutches, Ben and Bob on either side of him, supporting him. The twins' eyes were wide; they stood together between Basil and Joan, among equally wide-eyed children from the reserve. People from the commune were interspersed among the others; George beside Ben, David's dark-haired aunt near Mrs. Terpen.

"There is a power in a circle, and there is power in this night," said Naomi. "Let us use that power now as we think of Emily Hyde, to bring her spirit here one last time so that we may honour her memory." Naomi stepped away from the centre, taking her place next to Basil, reaching for his hand and for Trisha's. "Think of Emily," she said again. "Think of her, speak to her silently, ask her to join us here."

The centre of the circle grew misty, wavered, and there, alone on the freshly polished floor, alone, but close to those she now thought of as friends, stood the tiny ghost. She stood erect, looking gravely around her, standing as tall as a two-year old could.

"Welcome, Emily." Naomi spoke from the circle. "We bid you welcome here. We wish to bid you goodbye so that you may be released, may leave us, and freely, without sadness, go to where you want to be."

The small figure nodded seriously, as if she understood what Naomi was saying. "I think she does understand," thought Kelly. "Not the words, they're too complicated for her, but the meaning of the words."

Naomi spoke again, her voice deep, the words flowing from her in what was almost a chant, almost a song.

"Emily, small one,
We bid you welcome here.
Come, be with us,
Listen to us,
Share with us,
Know our love.
Know that you will be remembered,
Know that you are free to leave.
Come, be with us,
One last time."

She paused, then called to the twins. "Tommy, Trisha. Will you be the first to tell Emily good-bye?"

The twins, still holding hands, stepped forward and spoke together, spoke the words they had written and memorized as their farewell to the ghost-child:

"In the ghost place
Let there be Christmas every day,
Let there be candy and gum,
And your own T.V.
In the ghost place,
Let Emily have
Lots of happiness."

They stepped back into the circle, and Naomi smiled at them. There was a small cough, and Ben moved forward, a piece of paper in his hand. He read:

"May you be safe,
As the bulb underground,
As the grass, snow-mantled,
As the seed, earth-cushioned.
May you be safe."

He stepped back and, after a moment's hesitation, Bob took his place and spoke.

"I shall remember you
In the clay's softness,
In the sheen of the glaze,
In the yarn's strength,
In the glow of colours.
In all these things
I shall remember you."

It was quiet in the hall; the candles flickered, and the small figure in the centre of the circle nodded gravely. From his place between Ben and Bob, Ed Crinchley spoke, his voice rough and deep.

"I shall remember you
In the health of the young,
In the power of the river,
In the reading, in the books,
In the history, which is yours.
I shall remember you."

Clara Overton moved only slightly away from her place in the circle before she began to speak.

"May you be remembered
In the smell of fresh bread,
In the tart taste of rhubarb,
In the richness of cream,
In the warmth of coffee,
In an infant's cry. . ."

Her voice broke, and she stepped back, reaching for Father Glenn's hand. Basil took his turn, his feathered headdress swaying as he spoke, keeping the rhythm of his words.

"We shall remember you
In the salmon's high leap,

In the dancer's feet,
In the moving of the moon,
In the pulse of the drums,
In the rise of sacred smoke.
Be proud, small spirit,
We shall remember you."

As he rejoined the circle, the voices of his people came from where they stood. "Be proud, small spirit. We shall remember you," they echoed.

There was silence again. Naomi turned her head, her eyes searching out Alan Linden. "Will you, too, speak to her?" she asked.

He nodded, looking intently at Kelly for a moment before stepping into the centre of the circle.

"I will remember you, little one,
As the flowers blossom,
As the trees bear fruit,
As the machine runs smoothly,
As a daughter cries,
As a wife once smiled.
I will remember always,
Little one."

He took Kelly's hand again as he rejoined the circle, and she saw, reflected dimly by candlelight, tears moving slowly down his cheeks. Her father met her eyes, and the pressure of his hand, holding hers, increased.

David stepped forward, without letting go of Kelly's hand, and stood, half facing her, as he spoke to the ghost-child.

"May you be loved.
Always.
May you be remembered,
Always.

In sun-haloed hair,
In a smile,
In a laugh,
In a kiss,
In all my dreams.
May you be remembered,
May you be loved."

He turned so his last words were spoken directly to the still, silent figure in the centre of the circle, but Kelly knew that the words were for her as well. David bent and kissed her, then released her hand, placing it in the hand of Father Glenn, closing the circle as he stepped away from it. George, too, had left his place and now stood beside David, waiting.

"Now?" asked Kelly. David nodded, and George spoke softly, not disturbing the silence, the intensity of the rest of the group.

"We thought it best, Kelly. David's bus leaves soon."

"Good-bye, Kelly. I love you." David followed his uncle out of the hall, into the night. The candles flickered, the door closed softly, and he was gone.

"Kelly?" Naomi's voice startled her. "Kelly, will you say good-bye? Are you ready to do so?"

Kelly swallowed, and nodded. She dropped her father's hand and the young priest's hand, and took a step into the centre of the ring of people. In the candlelight, the small ghost's face seemed pale, almost frightened.

"Emily, little one," said Kelly, and moved closer to her ghost. The tiny figure in the red dress lifted her arms, her lips forming a hesitant smile.

"Kelly?" she said. "Bye, Kelly? Yes?"

Kelly dropped to her knees beside the child,

reaching out her own arms, feeling again the jolt of cold as she touched the small, outstretched hands. The candlelight caught the golden ringlets, burnishing them against the velvet bow which swayed slightly as the ghost lifted her head, looking at Kelly, silently pleading.

"Yes, Emily, good-bye. It is time for you to go, go home, be with your mother, be happy. It is time to say good-bye, Emily."

Still holding the small, cold hands in hers, Kelly spoke the words that she had written for the tiny ghost, the tightness in her throat easing as the words came, her voice growing louder as she spoke until it echoed through the hall, vibrant, strong.

"Emily, little one,
I say good-bye with love,
And I shall remember you
In the softness of a mother's touch,
In the twisting braids of hair,
In the gentling of a lover's kiss,
In all the farewells,
In all my farewells,
I say good-bye with love.
Good-bye, Emily."

She knelt, still holding the ghost's hands, and watched as the child lost her pale, frightened look and the tentative smile grew until the tiny face seemed to glow in the candlelight.

"Bye, Kelly. Bye."

Naomi began to speak again, and with her words, the ghost of Emily Hyde, two years old, began to fade, become misty, slip away.

"Go, Emily, go in peace.
Let the wind take you,

Let the water take you,
From this world
With your blessing,
With much love,
With gentle memories,
We ask you to be gone."

Naomi's words ended, the candles flared briefly, swaying as if moved by a wind that could not possibly have crept into the closed hall, and a thin curl of mist spiralled up into the darkness.

"Good-bye, Emily," Kelly said again softly. The tears began as she knelt there in the centre of the circle, kneeling alone, her arms still reaching out but now touching only emptiness. She knelt, and she cried.

"Good-bye, Emily. Oh, Mom. Good-bye."

Acknowledgements

This book would not have been possible without the following people who gave so freely of their time, their knowledge and their support.

Dave Jenkinson
Jean Kozocari
Members of the Alkali Lake Band
Robin Skelton
Dale Thomson
Father David Weir
Jean William

The Ghost of Soda Creek

Edited by Guy Chadsey
Cover art by Ron Lightburn
Cover design by Christine Toller
Typeset by Terry Worobetz
Set in Palatino (body type: 11.5/14.5)

This book was designed, typeset and prepared for printing electronically using Framemaker 2.0 and a QMS-PS 800 Plus laser printer.

Printed in Canada by Kromar Printing Ltd., Winnipeg.